"I'm going to put a stop to this!" Adam vowed

"You are? How?" asked Bridget.

"I don't know. I'm not sure..." he replied.

She smiled and trailed her pink bra over his chest. "Tell you what. You're a gambler, big guy. Let's make a bet."

"On what?" That smile was making him nervous.

"On you." She drew out the last word, teasing him. "Since you consider yourself my *friend*, you can give me an unbiased opinion on whether I'm good enough to make it as an exotic dancer. If you say no, I won't pursue my budding career."

"What? You want to do a demo for me?" His throat grew tight.

"Do we have a bet or not?" She definitely wasn't the shy girl who'd blushed when they first met as teenagers—now she wanted to take her clothes off in public? He couldn't let that happen. Her family would be horrified. He'd be horrified—no way was he letting any other male of the species catch a glimpse of sexy Bridget's beautiful curves and delicious peaks.

"It's a bet!"

Dear Reader,

My trip last year to Canada to meet my editors inspired the plot for *Bare Necessities*. On the way to Toronto, I stopped to see Niagara Falls. As I drove through town, I saw several signs for custom swimsuit designers and wondered where people went to swim. Niagara Falls is not a beach town and swimming the river is impossible.

Then I drove by several "gentlemen's clubs," and I realized that those designers had quite a different clientele. What if a self-conscious lingerie designer had a side job making outfits for exotic dancers? What if the dancers' outgoing personalities rubbed off on my shy designer and she decided to go after the man she's longed for since her teen years?

Bare Necessities also came out of my interest in how women view their bodies—often as imperfect inconveniences rather than the wonderful creations they are. My newly confident heroine grows to love her body—and she doesn't even lose a pound!

All the best!

Marie Donovan

P.S. I'm delighted to hear from my readers. Visit www.mariedonovan.com to enter fun contests and learn more about my upcoming books.

BARE NECESSITIES
Marie Donovan

HARLEQUIN®

TORONTO • NEW YORK • LONDON
AMSTERDAM • PARIS • SYDNEY • HAMBURG
STOCKHOLM • ATHENS • TOKYO • MILAN • MADRID
PRAGUE • WARSAW • BUDAPEST • AUCKLAND

ISBN-13: 978-0-373-79375-4
ISBN-10:   0-373-79375-8

BARE NECESSITIES

ABOUT THE AUTHOR

Marie Donovan, an award-winning author, is a Chicago-area native, who got her fill of tragedies and unhappy endings by majoring in opera/vocal performance and Spanish literature. As an antidote to all that gloom, she read romance novels voraciously throughout college and graduate school.

Donovan has worked for a large suburban public library for the past nine years as both a cataloguer and a bilingual Spanish story-time presenter. She graduated magna cum laude with two bachelor's degrees from a Midwestern liberal arts university and speaks six languages. She enjoys reading, gardening and yoga.

Books by Marie Donovan
HARLEQUIN BLAZE
204—HER BODY OF WORK
302—HER BOOK OF PLEASURE

To my sweetie pie. I'm glad you're better.

And to the staff of Children's Memorial Hospital. The work you do is the greatest love of all.

1

"HOW DO MY NIPPLES LOOK?" Sugar Jones craned her head around to check in the trifold mirror, her long blond extensions getting in the way.

Bridget Weiss brushed them aside. "Just a sec, I'll tell you when I'm done in the back." She finished pinning the silver bra band around Sugar's perfectly tanned, perfectly toned rib cage. A rib cage that carried a brand-new set of G-cup breasts, courtesy of a pricey suburban plastic surgeon and paid for by the slack-jawed patrons at Frisky's Gentlemen's Club, not a club that any *real* gentleman would belong to.

Sugar shifted from one foot to the other and circled the carpeted pedestal, her butt cheeks flexing in the costume's matching silver thong. Bridget bet she could bounce a quarter off those buns. The exotic dancer frowned at her reflection. "I don't think the doc got them quite even."

Bridget stared at the silver-spandex-clad breasts, as dispassionate as a pastry chef making sure her cake was frosted evenly. Sure enough, the left nipple was maybe a half inch higher than the right. At least they weren't off-center, like some other clients of hers. One girl had gone to a cheaper doc and wound up with a pair so asymmetrical, Bridget had found herself tilting her head in a futile attempt to see them as a balanced set.

But padding or a good pasty hid a multitude of sins. Even before starting fashion-design school here in Chicago last fall, Bridget had learned all the bra-design tricks in the book, plus a few more. "Let me pin up the left strap just a smidge."

She quickly made the alteration and Sugar smiled. "Much better. Now that I'm healed from my surgery, I'm going to be a feature dancer—finally a Frisky's Kitten!" She bounced up and down in her excitement.

Bridget backed away, not wanting to get biffed in the face by Sugar's frighteningly firm breasts. "A Frisky's Kitten, huh? That's quite impressive." She sincerely meant it. The stripper—rather, exotic dancer—business was as cutthroat a business as any of the high-pressure Chicago law firms or commodities trading partnerships that supplied most of Frisky's patrons.

Adam popped to mind, and just as firmly, Bridget tried to pop him out again. No such luck. She pursed her lips in aggravation. Adam Hale could do what he wanted, and if he wanted to lose a few brain cells and a lot of cash in Frisky's after a long day trading pork belly futures at the Mercantile Exchange, it was his business.

"Impressive and lucrative." Sugar closed one blue eye in a big wink. "According to the projections in my business plan, my implants will pay for themselves within eight to ten weeks."

"Business plan? Like spreadsheets and things?" What did Sugar do, calculate how many lap dances per night she needed to average? Bridget's business plan consisted of scraping together enough money to pay the large rent on her small apartment and grocery bill. Whoever thought you couldn't buy groceries for ten bucks a week just wasn't eating enough ramen noodles and peanut butter sandwiches.

"Spreadsheets, trend forecasts in the adult entertainment industry, the whole nine yards. I wrote my plan as a final project for my marketing class. I got an A-plus on it, too."

Bridget nodded. She couldn't imagine Sugar getting anything less.

"And my accountant thinks I might be able to write my implants off as a deduction on my tax return."

Wow, she needed a business plan and Sugar's accountant, as well. She had a hard time getting up the nerve to deduct basic things like fabric and thread. And heavy-duty silver spandex was not cheap. "Okay, I can have the bra ready for you the day after tomorrow. And I'll keep the pattern for your new measurements on file so you can call and order new bras whenever you need them."

"Great! I go through a ton of bras. Sometimes the customers grab them and won't give them back, or they land in a puddle of beer," Sugar complained. She unclipped the band and slung the bra to Bridget with practiced ease. "Oops! Thought I was at the club for a second."

Bridget didn't bat an eye as she folded the bra and set it next to her industrial sewing machine. Three months ago, the sight of another woman's breasts had made her blush hard enough to make her dizzy. Now even the extremely large pair a foot away from her face was simply another day at the office.

Sugar was shimmying out of the silver thong and into her civilian underwear, a plain black thong and ugly white cotton bra. She caught Bridget's surprised expression. "You know, I'm happy with my implants and all, but it's almost impossible to find sexy bras this size with good support. The straps are cutting into my shoulders and my back aches by day's end." Her glossy lips pouted.

"Tell me about it. That was how I got into designing lingerie." Bridget rolled her shoulders, stiff after bending over her sewing machine before Sugar's arrival. "I never found anything that fit me."

"I was wondering." Sugar gave her an appraising

look. "No offense, but you don't seem like someone with a background in adult entertainment."

"No offense taken." Bridget wasn't the type to inspire men to stuff money in her garter. With her light brown hair and pale skin freckled from too many summers hauling hay on the family dairy farm in Wisconsin, men were more likely to dismiss her as the younger-sister type. Like Adam.

"So no implants for you? And you must be at least a D-cup."

"Double-D actually and all natural, for better or worse." It had mostly been worse.

"Lucky! Do you know how much dough these set me back?" Sugar plucked at the plain white cotton bra.

Dough that she would make in less than three months of part-time work. Suddenly, Bridget was sick of ramen noodles and discount-store shampoo. She wasn't going to take off her clothes for money, but she could make more of an effort to build her business. "A great bra is essential for supporting large breasts or else they start to sag."

"Sag?" A look of horror crossed Sugar's face. "No one told me implants sag."

"Ah, but what about the skin holding them up?" Bridget nodded significantly. Especially skin that was already stressed by tanning booths and sprays.

Sugar put a protective hand over her bosom. "I never thought of that."

"Tell you what. I'll make you a nice, supportive, everyday bra and matching thong on spec. Your money back if it's not the most comfortable bra you've had. And you can keep the thong." She couldn't exactly resell a used thong.

Sugar paused from pulling on her white V-necked T-shirt. "A risk-free offer." She grinned. "I like it."

"Good." Bridget smiled. "What color would you like?"

"Ivory lace. And cut lower in the front so I can wear my plunging-neckline shirts."

"No problem." Bridget made a note on Sugar's client file. "So, I'll see you Friday at four when you come for the silver bra."

"Great." Sugar pulled on a pair of painted-on pencil-leg jeans and white ankle socks. She sighed as she tied her running shoes. "Stupid plantar fasciitis. My podiatrist says I'll need foot surgery unless I save my high heels for the stage. And dates, of course."

"No, those wouldn't work on a date," Bridget agreed. Not that she'd been on any in quite a while. "Unless you were going to the Cubs' game."

"True." Sugar got a speculative look on her face. "Or maybe I could choreograph a routine around my sneakers. An unbuttoned baseball jersey with a bra and thong underneath."

"With a team logo over each breast and one in the front of the thong," she suggested, half-jokingly. Although she could buy patches and appliqué them onto matching bras and thongs. Would the major-league franchises sue her if they found out? Probably nobody cared. Professional athletes were always going to strip clubs and they'd get a kick out of it.

"Brilliant! The baseball season openers are in a couple weeks, and I could wear a football jersey during the fall."

"Go Bears!" Bridget made a cheering motion. She was a Green Bay Packers fan herself, something she didn't advertise living only a few miles away from Soldier Field, the ancestral home of Chicago's favorite gridiron underdogs.

Sugar picked up her duffel bag. "Go money! That's what I cheer for. Speaking of…" She handed Bridget several bills. "Always get cash up front, that's my advice."

Bridget wrote a receipt and handed her the carbon duplicate. "To make your accountant happy."

"And I want to keep her happy. She used to dance at the Love Shack to pay for her CPA classes, so she knows the business inside and out. See you Friday." Sugar breezed out of Bridget's apartment and waved as she disappeared down the two flights of stairs to the quiet street.

Bridget returned to her working area. She'd only

been able to afford a one-bedroom apartment, so she'd turned her entire living room into her design studio and sewing room.

The room's corner was curtained off into a changing area. Most of her clients didn't bother to use it, not being the shy types. Her large drafting table faced the window to get the maximum light for her design sketches and pattern cutting. The trifold mirror and carpeted pedestal for fitting appointments were next to the huge sewing table with her machine on it.

Her sewing table was actually the old Ping-Pong table from her family's basement. It was big and sturdy enough to hold heavy projects like beaded wedding dresses, but had been a pain in the butt to move, needing Dad, her two brothers, Colin and Dane, and Adam to haul it into her third-story walk-up.

Adam had acted funny the whole time she was moving in, only talking to her when he needed to know where to set a box. It had been so awkward that she'd pulled Colin aside to ask him what the problem was. As usual, Col was clueless except to offer that Adam's girlfriend had made plans and wasn't happy that Adam had already agreed to help Bridget move.

A dutiful obligation. And that was just why she'd moved away from Wisconsin, from being Bob and Helen Weiss's baby girl and Colin and Dane's kid sister. She brushed some scraps of silver material and bits of underwire into her palm and threw them away.

She peered down her neckline as she bent over the wastebasket and saw a boring white bra. She also distinctly recalled pulling on discount-store cotton briefs that morning. Why didn't she take her own advice and wear something nicer? She'd left her family to go to fashion-design school in the big bad city exactly so she could create pretty, comfortable lingerie for women who were difficult to fit, large or small.

Bridget grabbed her sketchpad and markers. Sugar wasn't the only one who was going to get a sexy lace bra and matching thong. And whatever lucky man eventually got to see Bridget in lingerie wouldn't be thinking of her as somebody's little sister.

ADAM HALE CHECKED the number on his ringing cell phone. He sighed but answered anyway. He'd been ducking this call long enough. "Hello?"

"Hey, Adam, what's up?" It was Colin Weiss, his old college roommate.

Adam settled into his leather desk chair and minimized the futures trading window on his laptop. Colin was a bit of a talker, and Adam didn't want to get distracted during their conversation and accidentally buy high and sell low. No point in getting canned before he finished building his nest egg.

"Hey, Colin, nothing much. How are Jenna and the kids?" Colin had married his college sweetheart right after they graduated from University of Wisconsin-Madison and already had two rug rats.

"Fine, fine. In fact, we're expecting another one in about five months."

"Congrats!" Three kids, and he and Colin were only twenty-eight. Adam couldn't even imagine having one kid. Of course, he kind of needed to actually find a woman to settle down with first. He looked at the pile of work on his desk and realized the futility of that wish.

"Yeah, well, what can I say? She can't keep her hands off me."

"After a full day of chasing after a five-year-old and three-year-old?" Adam laughed. "You wish, Col. How's the farm doing?" Colin had majored in dairy sciences and had taken over his in-laws' small dairy farm a half hour away from his parents' farm in rural Wisconsin.

"Busy as hell, but you remember that from when you visited."

"Right." During those visits, they all worked hard. Adam, Colin's parents, younger brother, Dane, and Bridget, his younger sister.

As if he'd read Adam's thoughts, Colin brought

up the subject Adam wanted to avoid. "How's Bridget doing, Adam?"

"Fine, as far as I know. I stopped by her apartment a couple times to make sure she got settled and I've left her a bunch of voice mails." Bridget hadn't been home when he'd visited and she never returned his calls. Adam wasn't sure whether to be disappointed or relieved.

"Man, I wish she hadn't moved down there," Colin fretted. "She's a farm girl, sweet and naive. You know what those city guys are like."

"Almost as bad as you country guys," Adam retorted. "You weren't always the happily married father of three and you had plenty of stories to tell about those so-called sweet, naive farm girls."

Col grunted. "Bridget's different. I couldn't believe it when Mom and Dad let her move to Chicago to go to that fashion-design school. What was wrong with going to school at the university in Menomonie?"

"That isn't exactly Chicago, Col." Menomonie was in northwestern Wisconsin and its flannel-clad residents were not notably fashion-conscious. "Besides, Bridget's twenty-four, a full-grown woman." He veered away from that dangerous path. Col didn't need to know how much a woman he considered Bridget.

"She's only been home once in the six months

since she moved, and we hardly ever hear from her. Mom calls every week and we get occasional e-mails, but we don't really know how she is. You'd be doing me a big favor if you could see her, take her for coffee—"

"And report back to you?" Adam interjected. "She'll have *my* ass in a sling if she realizes I'm spying on her and then she'll come gunning for *you*."

"Please, Adam. Mom worries about her. She's the baby of the family, we only need to know she's okay."

He sighed. "All right, I'll call her and try to pin her down—" whoa, that brought some interesting images to mind "—for a time to take her out."

"Thanks, buddy. And if you could convince her to come home for a visit after her classes finish, I'll owe you big-time."

"You don't owe me anything, Col. You know that."

"Okay. But you should take some time off from your wheeling and dealing at the Merc and come for a visit, too. Maybe you can give Bridge a ride."

Adam gulped. "Sure thing. Talk to you soon." He clicked off his phone and rested his forehead in his hand. Pinning Bridget down, her soft, pale thighs spread wide beneath him. Giving Bridget a ride as she moved on top of him, her heavy breasts overfilling his palms.

His cock pushed against his zipper as he shifted

in his chair. How many futile erections had he sported over his best friend's kid sister? Ever since his senior year in college when he met her right after her high school graduation.

She had preferred to hide her amazing body under overalls and other baggy clothing, but they'd gone swimming once in the fishing pond behind the barn and his jaw had dropped. Fortunately, the water had been deep enough and his shorts baggy enough so Colin and Dane didn't notice his extremely inappropriate interest. Being bound hand and foot and thrown under the hooves of Caesar, the old family bull, would have definitely dampened his arousal.

After that, he only saw Bridget occasionally, like during Colin's wedding when they'd been paired as groomsman and bridesmaid. Sure, she was great-looking with her dark, almost navy-blue eyes and naturally sun-streaked hair, but he'd come to appreciate her dry wit and wry sense of humor.

The last time he'd seen her was when she moved to Chicago last August. He'd had a girlfriend then, but still reacted to Bridget the same way. What a jerk he was. And now Colin and the whole Weiss family were sending the fox to guard their precious chick.

BRIDGET WAS PUTTING the finishing touches on Sugar's order, the silver bra and brand-new ivory lace bra and thong. The dancer was coming over to pick them up. Hopefully, she'd love the new lace bra and order more. Now that Bridget had figured out Sugar's pattern, it was simply a matter of cutting the fabric and putting the bra together.

Her cell phone rang. Without checking the caller ID, she answered. "Hello?"

"Bridget?" A familiar male voice rumbled through her phone, startling her so she almost dropped it.

"Adam?" Her voice came out squeakier than she liked, so she forced herself to take some deep breaths.

"Hey, Bridge, how are you doing?"

Ugh, he called her Bridge just like her brothers did. Her nervousness dissipated. "Fine, keeping busy. Calling to check on me?"

"Um…"

Adam at a loss for words? He was *so* busted. "Colin or Dane?"

"Colin or Dane what?" He tried a valiant comeback, but failed.

"Was it Colin or Dane who called you and sicced you on me?"

He sighed. "Colin."

"Ah-ha!" Knowing she'd guessed right didn't make her feel any better.

"Come on, Bridge, they're concerned, rightfully so, that they don't hear from you as much as they'd like."

"First of all, if they heard from me as much as they'd like, I'd be calling down the stairs telling my mother what I wanted for breakfast every morning. Second, I'm an adult and don't need to check in with Mommy and Daddy all the time. How often do you call your parents?"

Adam didn't say anything. Bridget smacked her forehead in mortification. To quote her mother, who usually never had a harsh word for anyone, Adam's parents were dreadful. Bridget had plenty of worse words for them. "Look, I'm sorry, I shouldn't have said that."

"No, I'm sorry, Bridget. You *are* a grown woman and don't need someone who's not even family butting into your business."

"Adam, you know I consider you—"

"Like a brother?" His tone was sharper than usual.

"Oh, no. Two are plenty. But more like…" She couldn't think of a nice way to say she'd wanted to rip off his clothing and lick him all over ever since she was a teenager. "Like a friend," she finished lamely.

"A friend." He paused. "Well, as a *friend,* I'd like to encourage you to call home more often. You have a great family, believe me. They want to know how you're doing."

"You're right. But I need to prove I can do well here in Chicago since they were so dead set against it. I went to the local junior college and worked all kinds of goofy jobs to save my money for design school, and I'm finally doing what I want."

"I know you are, and I'm proud of you." His soft, silky voice sent shivers down her spine. He ruined the effect by asking, "How are you doing for money?"

"Fine." Sugar's voluminous bras caught her eye. There was her money right there. Funny, how everybody made money off two bags of saline. The surgeon, Sugar, Bridget, the strip club. Sugar's breasts were positively a cottage industry.

"You sure? City living is pretty pricey compared to Wisconsin."

"I'm fine, really. I even have a part-time job."

"Sounds good. Selling underwear again, like in that discount store?"

She latched on to that with relief. "Yes, I am selling underwear. To a very upscale customer base." She'd recently learned those buzzwords in her fashion-marketing class.

"Excellent. I know you must be busy, but if we could—"

Her call waiting blotted out his words. She checked and saw Sugar's number. "Adam, I have to go. One of my customers is on the other line."

"Customers? Why do they have your cell number?"

Uh… "'Bye, talk to you later!" She clicked over to Sugar. "Hi, how are you?"

"Hi, Bridget," she shouted over a crowd of female voices in the background. "I got called into work early and can't come for those bras. We'll have to reschedule."

"Oh. Okay." *Not* okay. Bridget needed that money. Bad. Her electric bill was due the next day, and as it was she was going to need to walk her payment into the currency exchange to keep her lights on and her sewing machine humming. "Wait! I'll drop them off for you."

"But, Bridget, I'm already at Frisky's. I don't want to make you come here."

"No big deal." She made her voice cheerful. "Just tell me where to go."

"Are you sure?" Sugar sounded skeptical. "This is a nice club in comparison to some other dives around here, but still…"

"Absolutely." Bridget was already packing Sugar's lingerie into her wheeled suitcase, along with some sample bras, thongs and corsets. She threw her sketchpad, colored pencils and some business cards on top. "It's a good opportunity for me to do some market research, talk about what you ladies need, learn what's in style right now."

Sugar laughed. "Bare skin is always in style, but if you don't mind coming, I'll introduce you to the girls. They're always bitching about not being able to find new outfits." The dancer gave her directions to the strip club. Bridget checked her bus map. It was only a short ride away.

"I should be there in an hour or so."

"Sounds good." There was a muffled shout in the background. "Gotta go, I'm next."

"Knock 'em dead." Bridget hung up and zipped the suitcase, almost giddy at her daring. The theme song from the *Mary Tyler Moore Show* popped into her head. She picked up a lime-green bra and flung it over her head, just like Mary's striped knit cap.

A little bit of Chicago business smarts and some Wisconsin stubbornness and she might make it after all.

2

BRIDGET HAD FOUND Frisky's. It wasn't hard, considering the ten-foot-tall, hot-pink neon kitten sign overhead. The kitten smirked at her in the twilight, its tail switching back and forth hypnotically. *Come have a good time, leave your money behind.*

Hopefully she was here to *get* some money. But where to find Sugar? She walked to the building's edge, peered around the corner and didn't see another entrance. There was probably a stage door for the dancers to use, but she didn't want to go poking around in a dark alley behind a strip club.

That left the main entrance. Bridget stepped into line behind some guys in expensive suits and overcoats. She ignored their curious stares, hoping the rising blush on her cheeks would be mistaken for reflected neon light.

The line moved quickly, and she found herself face-to-face with the club bouncer. He stared down at her, arms crossed over a fifty-inch chest. "Who ya here with?" he yelled over the pounding bass beat spilling out of the club door. The guys around her shrugged.

"I'm here by myself. I'm supposed to meet someone," she yelled back.

The bouncer looked even more forbidding. "Are you a new dancer? You wanna audition for the club?" He gestured to her suitcase.

She shook her head. "No, no, I'm not a dancer." Her self-esteem was bad enough without getting laughed off the stage.

"No single women allowed." He pointed at the sidewalk.

"Look, I'm not here for the show," she shouted. "I have something for Sugar."

"I got your sugar right here, baby," a man in line behind her called. Bridget gave him her meanest look. He just laughed and elbowed his friend.

She took a deep breath and turned to the bouncer. "Sugar, your brand-new Frisky's Kitten—" she pointed to the entrance "—is expecting me."

The guys behind her perked up. "Hey, you got a new Frisky's Kitten? Is she hot?"

"Tall, tanned and thirty-six G." Bridget figured Sugar wouldn't mind a little free buzz. A collective yelp rose from the line. "And if she doesn't get her special delivery, she might not go on for her second set!"

"Let her in, man! Thirty-six G!"

"Fine." The bouncer jerked his head at his co-worker to take over and tugged her into the club.

"Thank you!" she yelled over the pounding rock music.

"What?" He cupped his ear.

She gave him an exaggerated smile, figuring at least her white teeth would show in the black-lit club. He gave her his original grouchy look. After seeing the most beautiful girls in Chicago naked every night, her charms must fall flat.

And it was amazing that these girls didn't fall flat considering what they were managing in four-inch heels. There was a main-stage runway where one dazzling redhead did what could only be called a Little Bo-Peep show. She wore a tiny ruffled skirt and matching bonnet and not much else. Her toy sheep sat on the stage's edge as she did things with a shepherdess's crook that would make Mother Goose molt.

The club's corners held smaller stages where dancers held court, and several girls gyrated above men in private lap dances.

Her blush roared back. She could handle nudity, but the mock-sex made her all twitchy and embarrassed. She hurried behind the bouncer, eager to find Sugar.

Her escort took her through a hallway, past the kitchen and rapped on a door marked Private.

A towering brunette dressed in a mock-tattered

leopard-print slip opened the door. A dozen girls in various states of nudity rushed around behind her. Bridget gave the Amazon a weak smile. "Sugar's expecting me."

Her client pushed through the mass of tanned flesh, wearing a bright white bikini and matching superhigh heels. "Bridget!" She gave the bouncer a sultry wink. "Thanks, you're such a sweetie pie for making sure my personal designer made it here okay."

Sweetie Pie melted into a puddle. Bridget expected him to scrape his foot on the floor and say, "Aw, shucks." She must not have hid her amusement because he straightened in a hurry and glared at her. "Next time, go to the back door!" He puffed out his chest and headed to the front.

Bridget followed her client into the dressing, or rather the *undressing,* room. "Sorry, Sugar. But why won't they let women in? Surely you get some female customers here."

Sugar leaned into the lightbulb-surrounded vanity mirror and fluffed her blond extensions. "No, I'm sorry, Bridget. I should have told you to come around to the stage door. The bouncers have strict rules not to let unaccompanied women into the club."

"So the patrons don't bother me?" Bridget rolled her suitcase next to the vanity bench and peered over Sugar's shoulder. In comparison to the dancer's buffed perfection, Bridget looked like a schlump.

Her wavy, light brown hair had frizzed in the March humidity, and her summer-sun highlights had faded after a winter of city living. Her complexion was pasty and she had big rings under her eyes from staying awake late to finish her sewing projects.

"Um, so *you* don't bother the patrons. Not that you would, of course. Security's had problems with prostitutes hanging around, trying to pick up customers. Bad for business."

"Of course," Bridget said faintly, looking down at her suitcase. No wonder the guy had been suspicious. Who takes a suitcase to a strip club?

"Not that you look like a prostitute, or anything like that." Sugar patted her hand comfortingly.

That could be a compliment or an accidental putdown. Not skanky enough to be mistaken for a junkie hooker, or not pretty enough for a call girl? Bridget snapped out of her pity party. Whatever. Some women were meant to dazzle and some women were meant to supply expensive lingerie for them.

She unzipped the suitcase and lifted out the silver spandex and ivory lace garments. "I brought your bras."

"Wonderful." She took a cursory look at the silver one but ran her fingers over the ivory lace. "And this is my everyday bra?"

"Complete with gel-filled straps and special cup construction." Bridget was currently wearing a matching one in black lace. The matching thong and garter belt took a bit of getting used to, but she liked not having panty lines under the midcalf black skirt she was wearing. The getup hadn't boosted her confidence yet, but maybe it was a case of "fake it till you make it."

The leopard-print Amazon turned from where she was gluing on her false eyelashes. "So now you have your own personal lingerie designer? Well, la-di-dah!"

Sugar sneered. "Now that I'm a Frisky's Kitten, I can't afford to let these sag." She grabbed her breasts and thrust them at the other dancer.

Bridget intervened hastily. "I'd be more than happy to design something for you, as well. I'm Bridget Weiss, by the way."

"I'm Electra." The Amazon put down her mascara wand and shook Bridget's hand. Did she have a grip or what? If it weren't for Electra's feminine hands and lack of Adam's apple, Bridget might suspect there was more equipment under that outfit than met the eye.

"You have a very striking look. Very sexy and powerful." Bridget looked her up and down. Wide shoulders, black hair, thighs that could crack a walnut. Why not go with first impressions? "How about an Amazon costume? Kind of a gladiator outfit with gold over the breasts, gold cuffs and a fake sword."

"Or a real one for the assholes around here." Another girl sauntered over, wearing only a black leather thong and thigh-high black boots. She had a Goth look going, complete with inky hair, milk-pale skin, a pierced eyebrow and pierced…nipples? Bridget hadn't seen that in person before.

"This is Jinx." Sugar nodded. Next to Jinx, Sugar looked like a photo negative with her dark body and bleached hair. "She's our resident brainiac—a graduate student, no less."

"So what kind of costume would you design for me?" Jinx put her hands on her hips, daring Bridget to come up with something quick.

"Hmm." Bridget circled her, thinking frantically. Something tough, something dominant. "Remember the kids' comic book with the little devil in it? I'd update that for you with red boots, a pitchfork and headband with little sparkly horns. And for the main attraction, a red vinyl bustier with cutouts for your breasts. You could wear matching ruby nipple rings."

Where am I coming up with this stuff? she wondered. For a girl who started in lingerie design by adding tiny satin bows to her ugly old-lady bras, she sure was branching out.

Jinx quirked an eyebrow. "Sounds cool. Draw a sketch, and I'll take a look."

"Great." Bridget passed them both a business card and Sugar paid her the balance for the silver bra and the new ivory set. So it looked as if her electricity was good to go, and maybe she'd even splurge on some hamburger for her Hamburger Helper. Vegetarian Helper just didn't have much protein.

"Girls, you're up. Now!" a raspy voice bellowed across the room. A fierce old broad waved her clip-board.

"Marge is the house manager," Sugar explained. "She's been in the business for about ninety years and runs the show." She trotted away, her heels clicking.

The dressing room emptied. Bridget looked around. Was she supposed to leave or stay? She grabbed a disinfectant wipe and swabbed the Nau-gahyde couch. Maybe she could work up designs for Electra and Jinx now and leave with some more arranged commissions. Taking Sugar's advice, she'd get the cash up front. Money straight from the club customers to her, via the dancers' garters.

"HELL OF A DAY, huh, Hale?" Tom, one of his co-workers, leaned against the cracked vinyl upholstery of the cab they were sharing.

"The markets really took a beating." Several foreign countries had skipped their usual purchases of corn and wheat, raising supply and driving prices down. Fortunately, Adam had ducked the worst of it, but once he dropped Tom off, he'd go home and crash. Just like the markets.

"Thank God it's Friday. Sure I can't convince you to get a drink with me and some of the guys? We're meeting at Frisky's."

"Frisky's? I haven't been there in years." Strip clubs weren't his style anymore. He worked too hard for his money to blow it on overpriced drinks and overpriced dancers.

Tom laughed. "Hale, you sound like an old man, and you're fifteen years younger than me!" His laugh turned into a hacking cough. Adam decided not to point out that considering his coworker's bad habits, he'd be lucky to make it to old age.

They pulled to a stop in front of Frisky's, the pink kitten glowing in the dusk. A short line had formed. Adam hopped out of the cab to let Tom pass and saw a woman standing in line. He did a double take. Was that *Bridget?* Arguing with the bouncer at a *strip club?*

"Thanks for the ride, Hale. See you Monday." Tom pushed past him.

Adam gaped at the entrance. The woman disappeared into the club with a bouncer, but not before the pink neon clearly illuminated her profile. If that wasn't Bridget, it was her clone. He tossed some money at the cabbie. "Wait, I changed my mind."

"Sure, the more the merrier." Tom gaped as Adam rushed to the door.

Ignoring the protests of those already in line, he pushed to the front. "I need to get in there!"

"Don't we all, pal," the guy behind him said. "No line jumping."

The second bouncer pointed to the end of the line. "Sorry, sir, you'll have to wait your turn." He winked. "Don't worry, the girls are getting prettier as we speak."

That's what Adam was afraid of. "What about that girl who was just here?"

The guy behind him shrugged. "She said something about a new dancer named Sugar."

"Who's supposed to be superstacked," added his friend. "Now if you don't mind, it's our turn."

Adam's coworker dragged him to the back of the line. "Man, for a guy who didn't want to come to Frisky's, you sure are getting into it."

Adam smiled weakly, his mind churning. Was Bridget actually dancing at the club using the name Sugar? He knew she had to be on a tight budget, but this wasn't her style at all. She always seemed embarrassed about her great body, hiding it in baggy sweaters and her brothers' old flannel shirts.

Her brothers. Oh, *shit*. If she were stripping and Colin and Dane found out, they'd lead-foot it to Chicago and drag her back to Wisconsin faster than a cheap lap dance. And then they'd tie his body in knots around the stripper pole for not keeping her safe.

Finally, it was their turn. Adam paid his cover charge and followed Tom into the club. He scanned the smoky darkness for any sign of Bridget. When he didn't see her in the crowd of men and a few women, he forced himself to check the stages.

A quick scan found nothing but strange faces. He relaxed slightly, but still was apprehensive. Tom caught his elbow and steered him to the bar. "I'll have a Glenlivet Scotch, neat. What'll you have, Hale?"

Adam definitely needed to keep his wits about him. "I'll have a club soda."

Tom grimaced. "Club soda? Come on, you're allowed to live it up a bit at a strip club on a Friday night."

"All right, make it a Guinness." He hadn't had the dark Irish brew in a while. Tom rolled his eyes and paid an exorbitant amount for the probably watered-down Scotch, while Adam dug out money for his Guinness and some information.

He pushed a twenty toward the muscled bartender. "I'm looking for a girl."

The bartender nodded at the nude bodies behind them. "You're at the right place."

"No, not one of those girls." Adam checked the dancers again just to be sure Bridget hadn't appeared. "I'm looking for a specific girl—medium-tall, long, wavy brown hair with light-blond streaks, dark blue eyes and freckles. And a killer body," he forced himself to add, despite his embarrassment about speaking about Bridget like some jerk.

Tom set down his Scotch, his eyebrows raised. "Holy crap, Hale, you're never finding a girl here with all that going on—except for the killer body." He and the bartender traded grins. "I thought you were crazy when you dumped that swimsuit model you were dating last fall—what was her name?"

"Daria." Adam picked up his bottle and took a long drink of the dark beer. Unfortunately, the rich barley flavor didn't wash the bitter taste from his mouth.

"Yeah, Daria. She didn't look a thing like what you're asking for now. Didn't she have dark hair and eyes?"

Adam nodded. Daria had been dark to the core. Luckily he'd learned that before it was too late. "Are any of the girls named Bridget?"

The bartender shook his head. "These girls don't use real names. But feel free to keep looking." He turned to another customer and ended the conversation.

Tom nudged him. "We're not gonna find any girls if we sit on our asses at the bar. Let's go mingle."

Adam followed him into the middle of the club. A redhead with a stuffed sheep skipped off stage, replaced by an S-and-M-looking black-haired chick dressed in leathers and carrying a whip. No way that was Bridget, even with a wig. The Goth girl had much smaller breasts. Adam winced. Pierced nipples, too. Some guys must get into that scene, but definitely not him. He was more of a natural beauty connoisseur.

He'd lost Tom already. The other broker had sprawled onto a couch, a curvy Hispanic girl swaying on top of him. Judging from the glazed expression on his face, he'd be busy for a while.

Adam shook his head. Sure, he'd been young and dumb during his first couple of years at the Merc, going to his share of strip clubs with the guys. He'd enjoyed the attention from the dancers until he realized they were as good at trading as he was. Possibly better.

After all, they both sold possibilities. His were grains, livestock, something tangible. The dancers sold possibilities of themselves as girlfriends or lovers, a much more remote possibility. The corn crop always came in, but guys almost never hooked up with strippers. Those who did paid through the nose for the privilege.

The DJ changed the music to a sultry soul tune. "Let's all give a warm welcome to Sugar, our newest Frisky's Kitten!"

Adam choked midsip on his Guinness. That was the name Bridget had mentioned in line. What if it were Bridget, bared to the raucous crowd as she twirled on the stage? Jerks like Tom drooling over her creamy skin when *he* was the only one who should see her naked.

Wait, no one should see her naked, *especially* him. He turned in dread to the main runway.

A pair of shapely legs strutted out. As the dancer advanced, Adam caught sight of an extremely large pair of breasts. Not that he'd memorized her shape or anything, but he didn't think Bridget was *quite* that built. Finally the light hit the dancer's face. The knot in his stomach eased and he drank more beer. Sugar was pretty, but not as pretty as Bridget.

The catcalls and whoops grew to a deafening chorus as the Frisky's Kitten did her stuff. He caught some of her act as he continued to look around. Someone tapped him on the shoulder.

"Buy me a drink?" A muscular brunette ran her long fake nails along his arm. He took a double take. No, it wasn't a man after all. Maybe she knew something about Bridget.

"Sure." He ordered another Guinness and watched with a skeptical eye as the bartender poured something for the dancer from a bottle under the counter. Probably iced tea. He paid up and they sat together on a couch.

"I'm Electra."

"Adam."

"Your first time here? I would have remembered you." She gave him a sly wink.

"My first time here in a couple years. I wish I'd known what I was missing." He winked back. "My friend Bridget recommended this club."

"Bridget did?" She gave him a puzzled frown, glancing around.

"So you know her?" He mentally cursed his over-eagerness when he saw her withdraw. Great, now she thought he was a stalker. "I'm a family friend, just trying to make sure she's all right."

No luck. Electra finished her drink and gave him a tight-lipped smile. "Thanks for the drink." She gestured to his lap. "Unless you want something else, I should be getting along."

"No, no, thanks. But if you do run in to Bridget here, please tell her Adam's worried about her."

The dancer gave him a sarcastic look. "Sure you are." She stood and weaved her way through the crowd, stopping to smile at a skinny little man who couldn't take his eyes off her. Within a minute, she was rotating above him. Good thing her thigh muscles were strong enough to keep herself from crushing the guy.

It was obvious the girls weren't going to tell him about Bridget. They closed ranks to protect their own.

He circulated throughout the club, sipping at his beer until it became warm. No sign of Bridget. Maybe Tom knew where the dancers' changing room was. His coworker was pretty much blotto, stoned on a continuous supply of Scotch and female flesh, but managed to point to a hidden door next to the DJ's booth.

Adam set down his beer and casually made his way over to the door. When the DJ bent to pick up something from the floor, Adam ducked through. Three doors lined the fluorescent-lit hallway. One turned out to be a janitor's closet, the second was locked—probably the manager's office—but the third doorknob turned under his hand.

He opened it to face the S and M girl from the runway. She curled her lip. "Clear out before I call security to stomp your pretty face." It wasn't a compliment.

"Look, I'm here to see Bridget."

"No Bridget here." But like the tall brunette earlier, her eyes twitched briefly toward the back of the changing room. Years of working in the deafening trading pits had taught him to watch for tiny body language clues.

"Bridget!" he yelled. "It's me, Adam! I really need to talk to you."

"Get out of here!" The Goth girl actually picked up her whip and cracked it.

"Whoa." He raised his hands in a placating gesture.

"Sonny! Sonny!" the girl called.

The bouncer came running, alerted by the whip crack and her shouts. He stopped short when he saw Adam. "You again. Why can't you wait your turn and pay for a lap dance like everyone else?" He put his hand on Adam's arm.

Adam yanked away but bumped into the whip-wielding dancer. She planted her boot into the small of his back and shoved him to crash face-first into the doorjamb. The bouncer pinned his arm behind his back as the flesh under his eye stung and swelled. But it wasn't so swollen that he didn't see Bridget appear from the back of the dressing room. Her shocked, then disapproving, expression was clear as glass.

"Adam Hale. What the hell are you doing here?"

3

"TELL ME AGAIN WHY you insisted on bringing me home?" Bridget unlocked her front door and flipped on the light. Adam reached for her suitcase to carry it in but she glared at him and grabbed it herself.

"We need to talk." Adam followed her into her apartment, his cheek throbbing. He hadn't been there since her moving day. That heavy-ass Ping-Pong table held her sewing machine and several scraps of shiny material.

"Talk about what? How you got into a brawl with a stripper and were ejected by the bouncer?"

"Hey, I was not brawling with her. I lost my balance and she kicked me."

"You're lucky Jinx didn't crack you with her whip."

He shuddered. Totally not his scene. "That is one scary chick."

"What were you even doing there? I thought you finally grew up and stopped going to strip clubs."

"I did. And how do you know I used to go?"

She curved her face into a look of mock puzzlement. "Was it Colin or Dane I overheard bragging? Probably Dane, since he's single, and Colin isn't. Didn't you used to take Dane to clubs when he came to Chicago for business?"

"Damn. Those brothers of yours have some big mouths on them."

"You won't get any argument from me. So go home, and put some ice on your cheek." She pointed at the door.

Adam was halfway out the door when he stopped. Very slick. Her excellent offensive attack had almost distracted him from his own questions. He turned back to her. "I was dropping off a coworker on my way home when I saw you arguing with that bouncer. What the hell were you doing at a strip club?"

She paused from hanging up her coat. "The logical assumption would be that I am dancing at Frisky's."

He couldn't help himself and burst out laughing.

"Why is that so hard to believe? You don't think I'm sexy enough?" She glared at him. Uh-oh.

"Come on, Bridge. You, a stripper? You always wear the baggiest clothes possible and blush beet-red if anybody even glances at your—" He gestured abruptly at her breasts, too embarrassed to even say the word.

"Maybe I've changed since I moved to the city. Maybe certain things don't embarrass me anymore." She moved to her futon and picked up a shiny lime-green bra. "Don't you think this would make a perfect stripper top? Not that I would be wearing it all that long, anyway." She grabbed a matching thong off her worktable.

"Whoa, are you serious?" He ran his fingers through his hair. "You're dancing at Frisky's?"

She held the green bra to her chest and shimmied a bit. "What do you think, Adam?"

"Oh, my God." He looked, really looked around her apartment for the first time. A chrome clothes rack held a black corset thingie, a Day-Glo pink bra and panties, and a white vinyl tube top. No, that was a mini-mini-miniskirt. Bolts of silver, red and gold spandex fabric stood in a corner. But the kicker was a pair of six-inch clear plastic high heels with straps. *Nobody* wore those except strippers. "Did you dance tonight?"

She tossed down the bra. "Did you miss my performance, Adam?"

He laughed nervously and took off his coat. It was getting hot in her apartment. "Come on, I followed you into the club and I never saw you onstage."

"You're the strip-club expert, Adam. Don't dancers have private clients or do private parties?"

He plopped onto her futon. "Oh, Bridge. What will your family say?"

She just laughed. Here he was, picturing her parents' shock and horror and her brothers' anger and disappointment, and she *laughed?* She had changed since she moved to Chicago, and not for the better. "It's not funny."

"Adam, you worry too much." She plucked the pink bra off the hanger and rubbed her cheek over the shiny fabric. She'd look great in the pink with her fair skin....

"No!" He'd been imagining her in the pink bra and nothing else and hadn't meant to say that aloud.

"'No' what?" She gave him a puzzled look.

He jumped up from the futon and walked over to her. "No, you can't do that. Since your family isn't here, I'm going to put a stop to this."

"You are? How?"

"I don't know—do you need money? I can loan you some."

She looked shocked. All right, so he was tight with his money. Then she smiled and trailed the pink bra over his chest. His heart beat faster. "Tell you what. You're a gambler, big guy. You gamble on corn, soybeans, cattle. Let's make a bet."

"On what?" That smile was making him nervous. That and imagining how her breasts would look in the pink bra, her nipples hard against the tight fabric. Were they pink, too?

"On you." She drew out the last word, teasing him. "Since you consider yourself my friend, you can give me an unbiased opinion on whether I'm good enough to make it at Frisky's. If you say no, I won't continue my budding career as an exotic dancer."

"What? You want to do a demo for me?" His throat grew tight, and he reached to loosen his tie, only to remember he'd stuffed it into his jacket pocket hours ago.

"Do we have a bet or not?" Her blue eyes bored into him. She wasn't the shy little farm girl who'd blushed when they first met. And now she wanted to take her clothes off in public for strange men?

He couldn't let that happen. "It's a bet."

"Good." She pushed him toward the futon, and he sat uneasily. It reminded him too much of the couches at Frisky's.

She walked over to her CD player and bent over a stack of CDs, her breasts pushing against the front of her dark-blue blouse. Her firm ass was nicely outlined in the swishy black skirt.

He shifted uncomfortably. If her fully clothed curves were already getting to him, what would he do when he saw more?

She pressed the start button and stood. Marvin Gaye's song "Let's Get It On" started. Oh, no. Marvin was singing about holding back his feelings for a long time. Adam had tried, really tried to do the same, but now Bridget was swaying in front of him to the soulful music and all those smashed-down feelings and desires bubbled up.

She gave him a small smile and unclipped her hair. Waves of honey, coffee and gold tumbled around her shoulders. She shook them out and he gripped the futon's edge to steady himself, imagining those strands running through his fingers.

She squared her shoulders and looked like she took a deep breath. For courage? "Bridge, if you don't want to do this, we can cancel the bet."

Her confidence seemed to come roaring back. "First of all, don't call me 'Bridge.' It's a man's name." She reached for the top button of her blouse. "And I am definitely *not* a man."

No, she wasn't. Her fingers traveled down the column of buttons in an excruciatingly slow pace, giving him a peek at a black bra and flat belly. Then she shrugged her blouse onto the floor.

Adam's fingertips went numb digging into the futon, but that was the only thing numb. At the sight of her black-lace-clad breasts, his disobedient cock came to life.

Her skin was milky pale in contrast with the black lace, lush mounds of plump perfection curving above the bra. Even from where he sat in silent agony, he saw her nipples tighten against the fabric.

Her gaze dropped to his lap and her eyes widened in pleased surprise. He knew he'd lost the bet right then, but the fox side of him guarding the chicken coop wanted her to keep going.

And she did, swaying as she unfastened her skirt and dropped it to puddle around her ankles. He stared at her—from her sexy boots to her black lace garter belt, black sheer stockings and black lace panties. Oh, he loved black lace garter belts and black sheer stockings and black lace panties.

She kicked the skirt free and did a sexy little twirl, confirming his worst suspicions that her matching panties were indeed thong panties. Her ass was white and firm after years of physical labor and his fingers itched to dig into it.

She reached for the stocking hooks and he surrendered. "All right, all right, you win! You would make an absolute fortune at Frisky's." He would be her best customer. "But you just can't. Please, Bridget."

A broad grin crossed her face. "Not so fast. We're not done yet."

"Not yet?" It came out as a whimper.

"I don't think a striptease counts for the whole bet." She stalked toward him in her boots and lingerie and stopped between his widespread knees. He stared at her in a daze. Marvin was still crooning like crazy. "After all, the girls make most of their money on lap dances. Let's try it."

Adam's mind blanked. A platonic lap dance from the woman he'd lusted after for years? And just this evening he'd claimed not to be a masochist.

BRIDGET LOOKED DOWN at Adam, her hands on her hips. She'd thought she would feel awkward or embarrassed prancing around in fussy lingerie with her breasts and hips jiggling all over, but it was just the opposite. She was an all-powerful sex goddess, judging from the glazed expression on Adam's face. That, and the erection his finely woven wool pants couldn't hide.

No more little sister. She took a deep breath and knelt on the futon, straddling his lap.

Marvin segued into "Sexual Healing" and Adam groaned. "Bridge…"

He still didn't get it. "Bridget," she corrected, swaying over him. Although she wasn't touching him, the heat from his erection kindled a matching heat in her belly. And parts lower.

She shimmied closer, cupping her breasts and bringing them closer to his face. Her nipples were achingly hard, and she rolled them between her fingers through the lace.

His chocolate-brown eyes dilated at her daring and he swallowed hard. She reached behind her and slowly unhooked her bra, her gaze never leaving his. He gulped as her breasts spilled from the cups and she tossed the bra aside.

She paused for a second, letting him drink her in. Her nipples had always been extralarge, too, and she had tried to mask them for years with special adhesive covers or firm liners in her bras. But no more. Adam extended a finger toward one hard peak but stopped, still obeying the lap dance rules of no touching.

"Go ahead," she cooed. "You can touch me."

He looked up from her breasts, his expression serious. "If I do, I won't be able to stop."

"I won't want you to stop." And with that declaration, she sat firmly on his lap, his cock pressing between her thighs.

Their intimate contact broke his deadlock. To her surprise, he didn't grope her breasts, but instead grabbed her shoulders and pulled her into a kiss.

His mouth was hungry and gentle all at once. She responded eagerly, her tongue sweeping over the seam of his lips. With a groan of surrender, he finally opened to her, his tongue sliding along hers in a provocative dance. After so many years of lusting after Adam, their kiss was exactly what she'd hoped for and more than she'd dreamed of.

He pulled her even closer, and she ran her fingers through his hair. The black waves were hot silk under her fingers, and he made tiny noises as she massaged his scalp.

He broke free and ran kisses down her cheek and behind her ear. He clutched her to him, her bare nipples catching on his oxford dress shirt. She unbuttoned it with shaky fingers and spread the lapels wide. His chest was hard muscle and she rubbed her nipples through the black curls there.

He was heavenly. She ground against him, all finesse and pretense gone. His hands tightened on her back and he licked her collarbone. Was he reluctant to touch her breasts? Had he known how shy she'd been about them?

She pulled back and cupped them in her hands as an offering of trust. "Go ahead."

Instead of diving right in, he smiled at her and gently ran his index finger down her neck to one pink tip. His callused fingertip circled it slowly, around and around until she thought she might scream. "Adam…" He pinched her gently, and when she didn't flinch, he applied more pressure until she was twisting on him in sensual agony. Just when she thought that was the absolute best, he captured her other nipple with his mouth.

His tongue and teeth teased her, tormented her, tortured her. She was a prisoner of his hot, wet suction. Her nipples swelled even further under his expert caresses.

Exquisite sensation jetted between her legs, and her black thong grew damper. He hardened even more. She rubbed frantically on his erection, desperate to ease her ache.

As if he'd read her mind, he hooked a finger under the front of her thong and pulled it free. He insinuated his finger between her folds, driving through the soaking curls until he found his destination. He pressed her clitoris and she gave a short scream.

He grinned and her breast dropped from his mouth. He brought a hand to her leg and skimmed up and down. "I love these stockings." He stopped at the wedge of bare thigh above the seam. "But they're not as soft and smooth as you are."

"Oh, Adam." His sweet touch and his sweeter words overwhelmed her, and she turned her face away, a swath of hair protecting her emotions from his gaze.

She didn't have long to reflect before his finger rubbed her again. He circled her clit gently, then with more pressure, seeking every drop of her response.

Tension built under his hands, her thong adding its own sexy brand of friction where it rubbed between her bottom cheeks. She ground on him and clutched at his chest, his nipples hardening under her touch.

He made a choked-off groan. "Please, Bridget, make me stop before it's too late."

The sensual power she'd captured strutting around in her lingerie rose again. *She* was the one who could make him come fully dressed. *She* was the one who was taking control of her own sex life.

She cupped one breast. "Suck on me." And he obeyed.

His eyes closed as he eagerly feasted on her. His

hands stroked her soaking wet flesh and grabbed at her ass like they were grabbing for a life preserver.

He moaned in a low voice as she rocked on him. His arousal whipped hers to an unbelievable level. She tipped her body forward, and with her free hand reached behind her to grasp his balls.

His eyes flew open. She squeezed and caressed them through his thin wool pants. And since he was panting too hard to suck her nipples anymore, she decided to plant kisses on his forehead, his cheeks, his neck….

Her own tentative touches combined with his fingers and the thick cock under her twisted into unbearable tension. His balls pulled tighter under her hand. He gave one last savage thrust upward and she snapped like elastic stretched to the limit, pleasure rocketing from her clit to her breasts and deep into her core.

She gave quiet cries of pleasure and triumph. For years, Adam had been her schoolgirl fantasy as she'd furtively brought herself to release, but the reality was much, much better.

Adam yanked her close and rubbed his cock on her, his face pulling into taut lines. "No, Bridget, stop, ahhh…" But she gave his balls one last squeeze and he came hard, gasping and squirming, his breath hot and fast against her aching breasts.

Bridget slumped against his shoulder, his heart thudding under her touch. For a minute, she just cuddled, then stroked his silky chest hair. She'd longed to do that since his first visit to the farm and she saw him tossing hay bales without wearing a shirt. But their tender moment didn't last long. She knew the second he started regretting what they'd done.

He squirmed underneath her, and not in a happy way. "Oh, man. Oh, man." He hooked his hands under her arms, careful to avoid her breasts, and she climbed off him.

She sprawled onto the futon next to him, feeling like a pinup with her garter belt and boots still on. Now if she got Adam into the bedroom, they could go for round two.

He hopped up from the futon and made a beeline for the bathroom, not the bedroom. Well, that was okay. He did need to clean up and maybe they could take a shower together.

Pulling herself off the futon, she strode across the living room. Give her a whip, and she'd match Jinx. Except for the pierced nipples, of course. She tapped on the bathroom door. "Adam?"

He didn't answer, so she tried the door. He'd locked it? "Adam, are you okay?" She jiggled the doorknob.

"Fine." He didn't sound fine. "Bridget, I need a pair of pants."

"Oh. Okay." She went into her bedroom and caught a glimpse of herself. Her hair was beyond mussed, but there was a gleam in her blue eyes and a rosy blush to her skin. If she refused to get him pants, would he stay?

Although a naked Adam trapped in her apartment appealed to her very much, she rummaged through her dresser and found an old pair of gray sweatpants that were too long for her. Maybe they'd fit him.

She returned to the bathroom and knocked. "Here you go." He opened the door far enough to grab the pants and then locked it again.

Suddenly feeling chilly and not much like a pinup anymore, Bridget went into her bedroom and pulled on her fluffy sky-blue chenille bathrobe. The fabric brushed her sensitized skin and she shivered.

She heard the bathroom door open and hurried out. She fought back a giggle at his outfit. The pants were still too short and showed a chunk of bare, hairy leg above the tops of his black socks and dress shoes. When she saw his face, though, she stopped laughing.

He looked absolutely grim. "What's the matter?" She already knew the answer.

"What's the matter?" His eyebrows shot up. "We just did all this, and you ask what's the matter?"

"I don't know." She shrugged. "It felt pretty good." *Good* was an understatement. Hedonistic, ecstatic, orgasmic—yeah, that last one covered it.

"I lost the bet." His expression grew even darker. "Now you know just what power you'd have over those poor slobs at Frisky's. If I were your customer, I'd wipe out my savings, max out my credit cards, sell a kidney to have you naked on top of me."

"Wow." That was quite a compliment. Too bad he looked as if he were donating his kidney. Without anesthetic.

He grabbed her forearm. "Think about your family."

"Are you going to tell them I'm a stripper?" If he did, she might have some explaining to do about sewing lingerie, but that was all.

"No, I don't want to hurt them." He assumed a noble expression. "You're their baby girl."

She grimaced at him, exasperated. "All the dancers at Frisky's are somebody's baby girl." Except for Electra, who was possibly someone's baby boy.

"Then think about yourself. Those strippers will only drag you down to their level with their bad habits—alcohol, drugs."

"In the first place, the dancers drink watered-down liquor at work so they don't get tipsy and hurt themselves. And the only thing they inject into themselves is lip collagen." She crossed her arms over her chest. "Half go to school, the other half dance to support their kids. Sugar is working on her business degree and Jinx told me she's working on her master's thesis in comparative lit at Chicago University."

He shook his head. "Forget about my weakness for you, Bridget. You know this is a bad idea. Promise me you won't dance at Frisky's until we talk again."

He had a weakness for her? Well, vice versa, Adam. "I don't know…." She pretended confusion until she saw his anxious expression. "All right, I promise. I won't wear sexy lingerie and take it all off at Frisky's for a man who'll beg to see my bare breasts swaying in front of his face. And I definitely won't wear my garter belt and stockings to give anyone a lap dance so that he's squirming under me from sheer arousal."

He swallowed hard. "Fine." His voice squeaked and he tried again. "Fine. Thank you, Bridget. You're an old-fashioned girl. You don't belong doing *any* of that."

Oh, yeah? Bridget gave him a tight smile. The next time she saw him, this old-fashioned girl would do things the old-fashioned way and take him *all* the way.

·

4

"ADAM SAID WHAT?" Electra reached for the plastic sword stuck in the waistband of her Amazon costume as if to run him through.

Bridget lifted her glass of champagne in a weary toast from where she reclined on her futon. Was it her second or third glass? She couldn't remember. Probably a bad sign. "He said I was an old-fashioned girl who shouldn't be giving him a lap dance."

"He's totally repressed." Jinx snorted. She stretched on the other end of the futon in sweatpants and a black punk-rock T-shirt. Her brand-new red vinyl devil costume was tossed over a nearby chair.

"He never used to be," Bridget complained, sucking down more champagne and raising her glass for another refill from Jinx. "My brothers used to brag about how wild he was, hopping from girlfriend to girlfriend, blowing money at strip clubs."

"He's not a regular at Frisky's, anyway," Sugar

commented, twirling in front of the mirror to get a better look at her royal-blue Chicago Cubs bra-and-thong set. "I'd remember him."

"Or at least what his wallet looked like," Jinx cracked.

"One time in college he even had a threesome with two cheerleaders." Bridget had been jealous but aroused when she'd overheard that gossip, imagining him spread out on a bed, his silky hot skin licked and caressed….

She hadn't had the chance to do any licking and precious little caressing. Why should two greedy cheerleaders get all the fun?

She stared moodily into her champagne. Heavy drinking was probably a dumb idea at three in the morning, but the dancers had just finished their shift and wanted to pick up their new costumes. Along with Bridget's rent money, they had brought a few bottles of contraband champagne.

"What are you gonna do now?" Electra pulled on the breakaway tabs of her golden breastplate and shrugged it off. She'd had implants as well, but in a more modest size to better fit her more muscular build. Electra had told Bridget that she'd been a highly ranked track-and-field athlete until she'd blown out her shoulder shot-putting.

Maybe Electra would shot-put some sense into Adam. "I don't know what to do. After what we did together last weekend, he can't still possibly think of me platonically."

"There's no such thing as platonic between men and women. Every man has his breaking point. You just have to find it." Sugar carefully hung her Cubs lingerie and matching ball cap on a padded satin hanger she'd brought from home.

Bridget frowned. "Breaking point? That sounds kind of violent."

"Some guys like that." Jinx gave her a sly smile and caressed the red whip she'd bought to go with her new outfit. "Big, bossy men get a taste of this and beg for more."

"I don't want to break him, I only want to…"

"Screw him?" Sugar added, gliding over for another glass of champagne.

Bridget blushed.

"Same thing." Jinx shrugged.

Bridget yanked up her shirt to show them her new red lace bra. "Do I look old-fashioned? Do I? I even have the matching thong on, too." She stood to show the dancers, but got dizzy and plopped on the futon.

"Yeah, you're a real wild one, Bridget." Jinx rolled her eyes.

Sugar thoughtfully tapped her acrylic, French-manicured nail tips on her glass. "Let's dress her up."

"Like what?" Electra glanced at the red vinyl

outfit. "Our regular dancer outfits would make her self-conscious."

"The guy has a point—she has that kind of girl-next-door, take-home-to-mommy look. Something classy, yet sexy," Sugar pronounced. "What do you think, Bridget?"

Bridget blinked. She'd been daydreaming about Adam. "That's me, classhy and seckshy." Funny, her mouth didn't seem to be working right.

Jinx sat upright. "I know, I know. *The Age of Innocence.*"

Her suggestion met with guffaws from the other two dancers. Electra said, "Honey, none of us has been that age for a long time."

"Not that, you ignorant bimbos. I mean the book *The Age of Innocence.* Edith Wharton's novel about upper-class New Yorkers in the late eighteen hundreds?" Jinx heaved a sigh of exasperation. Her grad school tuition in literature at Chicago University was very expensive, just like Jinx. By dancing at Frisky's, she made more than her professors and had no student debt, as well.

"It was a movie, too," Bridget volunteered. "Daniel Day-Lewis, Michelle Pfeiffer and Winona Ryder. Lotsa cool coshtumes."

Sugar nodded. "Oh, right! His character was having an affair with Michelle even though she was his girlfriend Winona's cousin. Winona's character took him back."

"I had a guy do the same exact thing, except it was my sister he was banging," Electra offered. "Only I didn't take either of them back."

Silence fell over the room. Electra didn't look particularly upset, though.

"*Anyway,*" Jinx said, clearing her throat, "think corsets. Think stockings. Think crotchless drawers."

"They had those back then?" Electra looked impressed. "Who woulda thought?"

Jinx hopped up and flipped through Bridget's clothes rack. Sugar came over to the futon and unclipped the barrette on the back of Bridget's head. "Let's see this clump of hair."

"Hey!" Bridget batted her hand away. Sure, her hair was messy. But if people wanted to visit at 3:00 a.m., they took their chances.

Sugar ignored her and rubbed a few strands between her fingers. "It's actually in pretty good shape. When was the last time you had a deep conditioning treatment?"

"Um, never. Except for when my hair got really fried in the summer and I put mayonnaise on it."

She shuddered. "Here in the big, bad city, you can actually buy conditioner that doesn't make you smell like an egg-salad sandwich. But for now, you really need some color."

Bridget sighed. "I bought a box of highlights but haven't put them in yet." She pulled herself off the futon and dug the hair-color box from the linen closet.

While Sugar examined the box, Bridget gave a jaw-cracking yawn. "Maybe some other time. I've only had a few hours' sleep…."

Jinx clattered the hangers and turned to her. "I can understand if you don't want that guy Adam. He acted really wimpy when I cracked my whip and kicked him in the ass. Never even tried to hit me or anything."

Bridget straightened from her slouch, her sleepiness gone. "He is not wimpy! He would never harm a woman, that's all."

Sugar waved the highlights box. "Do you want him enough to put some effort into it? If you sit back and wait for good things to happen to you, you'll be waiting a long time."

"And you think highlights and corsets will do the job? It seems so superficial." As soon as she said it, she felt foolish and a little sad. These three women spent tons of time and money on costumes and cosmetic improvements.

The dancers exchanged glances. Finally, Electra sat next to Bridget and patted her hand. "It's not so much about how you look to other people. It's how you feel to yourself. The girls and I, we use our hairstyles and outfits to tap into that small part of our inner selves that we're willing to share with the patrons when we dance. I wear the warrior-girl outfits because I'm a jock, Jinx wears the bondage stuff because she likes to boss men around and Sugar wears those giant boobs because she likes to be the absolute center of attention and a real stage hog."

Sugar gave her a smug look. "And I have one implant paid off already."

Electra gave her an arch look. "I thought you were looking a bit lopsided." She laughed as the other dancer stared at her chest in dismay.

Jinx shrugged. "Okay, Bridget wants this dude for whatever reason, so let's get her hair done, get her dressed and get her laid."

"Jinx." Bridget shook her finger at the dancer, but her giggles ruined the scolding. If her stripper fairy godmothers could help her land Adam, she'd tolerate some fussing over her appearance. "Okay, let's do it."

Sugar whooped with glee and shoved another glass of champagne into Bridget's hand. "Drink up, sweetie. Looking beautiful is never easy."

BRIDGET ROLLED OVER in bed and groaned as sunlight blasted her closed eyelids. She rolled back and cracked open an eye to check her clock. One-fifteen? She'd never slept this late in her life. She bolted upright and immediately wished she hadn't.

She rubbed her aching temples and found unfamiliar curls there. Oh, no. She vaguely remembered some drunken hairstyling. At least, *she'd* been drunk. She hoped that Sugar hadn't been.

Crawling out of bed, she braved a look in her dresser mirror and shrieked. Ignoring the bloodshot eyes and pouches under them big enough to fit a C-cup, she desperately fluffed her crushed hair.

After a panicky minute, she'd figured out what Sugar had done—cut her wavy hair into layers short enough to get some curl but leaving it long enough to pull into a clip if she needed. Subtle blond highlights emphasized the new cut. Even her face looked different and she couldn't tell why. She examined it closely and found her eyebrows plucked and lightened.

She winced. Now she remembered the plucking. Jinx had done that, of course, with great enthusiasm. Bridget was lucky to have escaped a drunken Brazilian wax. She double-checked in case her memory failed her. Okay, no surprises there.

She pulled on her robe and made her way into the kitchen. A note sat on the tiny bistro table.

Hey, Bridget, hope you like your new look. Jinx says to make some crotchless drawers, put on that black corset and go get your guy. Remember, shoulders back, chest out and smile! Sugar.

After signing her name, she'd drawn a big smiley face.

Bridget fixed herself some tea and cinnamon toast to munch on while she contemplated her plan of action. She wanted Adam more than ever since their passionate encounter, and it was obvious he didn't think of her as a little sister anymore. He'd even admitted it, albeit grudgingly.

She'd already decided to tell him the truth about her nonexistent stripping career. Her playacting had broken the ice between them, but she didn't want to continue deceiving him any longer than necessary.

Dialing Adam's number, she fought back nerves until it clicked over to voice mail. She pursed her lips. "Hi, Adam, it's me. I've been talking to some girls at Frisky's about dancing there and I really need to see you. Call me." It apparently *was* still necessary to continue her charade.

As she expected from her truthful yet provocative message, her phone rang within two minutes. "Bridget, no," he said without preamble. "I don't care what they tell you, the money's not worth it. I'll loan you—"

She broke in to his speech. "Hello to you, too, Adam. And I haven't danced there yet."

"Oh. Good."

"But I want to discuss all of this with you in person. I'll be at your place at six."

"Here?" His voice rose in surprise. "Can't we meet somewhere for coffee? Somewhere public?"

"No. Besides, I've never been to your apartment before and I'd like to see it."

"I don't know, Bridget...."

An unwelcome idea crossed her mind. "Do you have a new girlfriend? Someone who might not be happy to have me there?"

"Hey!" Now he sounded angry. "I may not have been on my best behavior the last time we met, but I would never have done um, *that,* with you if I had a girlfriend. Despite what your brothers may have told you, I've never cheated on anyone, not even in college."

She smiled in satisfaction. She had the playing field all to herself. "Do you have plans tonight?"

"No, but—"

"Now you do. I'll be there at six. Bye." She hung up quickly and giggled as her phone rang immediately. Pressing the button to send Adam to her voice mail, she jumped up from her kitchen table. She had a pair of crotchless drawers to sew.

ADAM RUBBED HIS TEMPLES, the familiar pounding starting again. His doctor had warned him that his blood pressure was creeping into the dicey level. He'd be popping beta-blocker pills to drop it unless he was careful.

He was reaching for his battery-operated blood-pressure cuff when his phone rang again. It was his father. Duty warred with self-preservation. Well, crap, may as well get it over with. He sighed and answered his phone. "Hello?"

"About damn time you picked up. Too fancy to have a regular house phone like everyone else, Mr. Hotshot only has his cell-you-lar phone."

"Hi, Dad." Like they didn't have cell phones in Wisconsin. He let his dad's criticism slide off his back. The old man would simply twist everything he said anyway. "How are you doing?"

"How am I doing? How am I doing? I'm doing awful, that's how."

What else was new? Billy Hale had been complaining of doing awful since Adam could remember. "Sorry to hear that." He was especially sorry he hadn't let the call go to voice mail.

"It's that damn IRS. They did some audit thing and claim we owe them money."

"The IRS?" Adam sat up straight. "You got audited by the IRS? When was that?"

"Right after New Year's. Said something about not reporting income on that herbal-type business your ma was running. Damn herbal company was shut down by the Feds anyway, and then they got the goddamned nerve to say we owe 'em taxes on that dough."

Please, no. "What herbal company?" He was

afraid to ask. Had they been growing pot in the closets again? They'd refused to talk to him for months after he destroyed all their plants. It had actually made his eighth grade year easier.

"Yeah, your ma was making a killing selling herbal supplements to the local college students so they could do all their fancy studying and the FDA comes in and says those herbs are dangerous. Just 'cause some wimps got their hearts goin' funny from it. So we figure, screw it. Those Feds wrecked the business, they damn well don't get their damn taxes from it."

"But now they want their money because not paying taxes on purpose is considered tax evasion, and they can send you to federal prison for that."

His dad scoffed. "They ain't sending us nowhere, especially since I told them I could pay their taxes plus some big-ass fine."

His stomach churned. Finally they came to the real reason for the call. "How much money?"

His dad nonchalantly named a figure that made Adam blanch. For a second, he was tempted to hang up and let his parents dig themselves out of their own mess. But despite the fact that he would have been better off being raised by a pack of wolves, he didn't really want them sent to the federal pen in Oxford, Wisconsin. "I'll send you ten grand. That should get them off your back for a while, anyway."

"Sonny, that ain't gonna be enough. I know you're making more money there than the federal mint, so you oughta send me and your poor ma more than that."

Adam clenched his fist. "Ten grand is a bundle. Besides, that's all the liquid cash I have. The rest is tied up in investments."

"Well, Mr. Fancy-Pants, untie it, or your ma's gonna be tied up at the police station."

"Hey, Dad, why don't you sell that vintage Harley of yours? I bet that would cover the rest of your tax bill."

"Bite your tongue, boy. That Harley leaves my possession the day they plant me in the ground. Or maybe I'll be buried with it just to spite you."

His father lived his whole life to spite him. "Ten thousand bucks. Take it or leave it."

"Fine. Overnight me the check, will ya?"

He laughed. Despite what his father thought, Adam was no fool. "I don't think so. Get me the agent's name and your case number. I'll pay the IRS and nobody else."

His dad grumbled but gave him the information. Adam would call the IRS Monday to make sure this was on the up-and-up, at least so far as tax evasion and heart-damaging illegal herbal supplements could be considered on the up-and-up. He wouldn't put it past his father to rig some elaborate swindle.

"And don't dawdle, sonny. Them Feds are mea-

suring me and your ma for jumpsuits as we speak."
His dad hung up with a click.

"You're welcome," Adam told the silent phone.
He turned it off altogether and dropped it onto his
leather couch. No more phone calls today. First
Bridget with her outrageous idea of taking her
clothes off for money, and then his dad demanding
money to stay out of jail.

He thunked his fist onto the couch and swore.
The blood-pressure machine slid to the carpet. He
didn't even want to know what it would register now.
How was he going to loan Bridget money to keep her
out of trouble and his parents, as well?

He hadn't been lying to his father when he told
him almost all of his money was tied up in investments. A little voice in the back of his mind told him
to forget his parents for once and let them answer for
their own actions, but he shrugged it off. He'd bail
them out one last time, and that was it.

And as for Bridget, he'd take an advance on his
credit card if she was in a jam. After finally seeing her
naked and twisting passionately above him, there was
no way he was letting her do that for other men.

He jumped to his feet. His place was in no shape
for visitors and Bridget would be coming over in
a few hours.

A stack of take-out menus caught his eye. Bridget
probably wasn't eating well, either. His regular

Italian place could deliver a nice meal. Colin and Dane would appreciate him taking care of their sister. In the kitchen, not the bedroom.

5

"THANK YOU FOR ORDERING in such a nice dinner, Adam. It was so thoughtful of you." Bridget smiled at him as he slid a plate of pasta onto the black place mat in front of her.

"Sure." Thoughtful, huh? He was having trouble keeping any thoughts in his head that didn't involve chucking the nice dinner down the disposal and carrying her off to his bed. His freshly made bed with nice, clean sheets. He sat across from her in a hurry.

Their knees bumped under the narrow dining table. She shifted slightly so one of his knees was between hers. He scooted away, but was about eighteen inches from his plate. He moved in casually, careful to avoid her legs.

Although hidden by the light wood tabletop, her legs were fresh in his mind. She was wearing a tight black skirt with high-heeled shoes and stockings that actually had a seam along the back. He reached for his wineglass and gulped half.

Maybe he should have forgotten the white wine. He knew he needed to keep a clear head around her, especially when she was wearing the softest, fluffiest red sweater he'd ever seen, dipping between her breasts to showcase several inches of pale cleavage. He wanted to pet her like a kitten and bury his face in that deep, deep V. Sweat trickled down his back despite his short-sleeved black button-down shirt.

Bridget gracefully twirled her fettuccine Alfredo around her fork and popped it in her mouth. She chewed and swallowed, a blissful expression on her face. "Delicious." She gave him a smile and gestured to his plate. "Eat before it gets cold."

"Oh. Right." He turned to his meal and forced himself to eat. Although it was delicious, he couldn't relax. Her auditioning at Frisky's still hung over their heads. At least over *his* head. She looked perfectly content. Had she made her decision already? If so, what was it?

He was about to ask when she spoke. "How is work?" He watched in fascination as she slowly wrapped another creamy fettuccine noodle around her tongue. "Adam? Adam?"

"What? Oh, work." He stopped to collect his thoughts. "Busy. Almost too busy."

"Too busy? Are you having trouble?"

"Not exactly."

Her gaze focused over his left shoulder. "Is that a blood-pressure cuff on your counter?"

Crap. He'd forgotten to toss it in the closet when he was cleaning his place.

"You have high blood pressure, don't you?" She set down her fork. "Oh, Adam, you're only twenty-eight. What on earth is going on?"

"Just a glitch. Too much junk food, chips, pretzels, you know."

She narrowed her eyes. "A guy your age should be able to eat all sorts of garbage and not have blood-pressure problems. My dad didn't get high blood pressure until he was in his fifties."

"Gee, thanks." Now she was comparing him to her dad, a man who ate at least ten pounds of meat and eggs a week and whose wife had only recently stopped cooking with lard.

Bridget looked at her plate of pasta. "You don't usually eat like *this,* do you?"

He shook his head. "No, no, not at all." Usually, it was worse. The hot-dog vendor on the corner near his office knew him by name and asked about him in concern if he missed a day.

"Good. After today, it's low sodium and plenty of fruits and veggies. If it doesn't get better, you need to think about changing jobs. You were the one who told me the commodities pit is brutal and traders can burn out by their thirties."

He rubbed the back of his neck. "Well, yeah, that's happened to a couple guys I know, but it won't be a problem for me. I have a plan to retire in a couple years once my finances hit a certain point."

"Really? That's wonderful. What will you do after you leave the pit?" She scooped a bite into her mouth.

"I'm going to buy a farm." He grinned at her. She was the first person he'd told besides his financial planner.

Her fork froze between her lips as she gave him a wide-eyed stare. She pulled the fork free and hastily chewed and swallowed. "A farm? You want to be a farmer?"

"Yeah. I'll buy a medium-size spread in Wisconsin. Fresh air, green grass, rolling hills—the whole package. I'll move there and never want to leave. Just like your dad and brother."

JUST LIKE HER DAD and brother? Bridget realized her mouth was hanging open and closed it with a snap. She finally got off the farm and the man she wanted most was planning to run back to it. If he thought his blood pressure was bad on the trading floor, he should see what it would be like running a farm. Especially a dairy farm. "What kind of farm were you thinking of, Adam?"

"Dairy, of course."

Of course. What other kind of farming did he

know? "Don't count on fresh Wisconsin breezes. You know that old joke—'Wisconsin: Come Smell our Dairy Air.' It's true, you know."

"Of course I know that." He smiled. "I have worked on your dad's farm before."

"Yes, yes, you have." She forced a smile at him. He'd spent exactly one week there and Colin and Dane had pretty much given him menial tasks to keep him out of the way and prevent him from getting hurt. "Do you have any other farming experience? Maybe from your internship in college?"

He shrugged, looking slightly embarrassed. "Not really. My internship was with the American Honey Export Association."

"Honeybees?" She stifled a giggle. "Maybe you could be a beekeeper instead. They don't need milking twice a day."

"Don't be silly, Bridget." He made a face. "The office was in Washington, D.C., and the only bees I saw were three-foot-tall photo enlargements on the office walls. It was months before I ate honey again. Nope, once I saw how happy you all were working on your dairy farm, I knew that would be the life for me."

His earnest tone melted her heart. "Oh, Adam." She reached over the table and grabbed his hand. "Please, do me a favor, though. Before you buy any land, go live with my parents for a few months and really work on the farm. Do it in calving season so you get a real feel for it."

"Good idea. Your dad grew up on the farm. If there's anyone who can show me the ropes, it's him."

"That's true." Bridget ate another mouthful of pasta and chewed thoughtfully. Adam had grown up in a rough blue-collar neighborhood of Milwaukee, so it was no wonder the bucolic farm life seemed appealing. If he still wanted to farm after shoveling tons of manure and sticking his arm shoulder-deep into a cow's birth canal, more power to him.

Not for her, though. She'd literally scraped the Wisconsin farm soil from her feet and was on her way to making it in the city. She finished her glass of wine and reached for the bottle to pour them both more.

"Thanks for listening to my goofy plans, Bridget. I haven't told anyone else because they'd think I was crazy." He gestured around his condo. "Leaving a good job and my nice place to move to rural Wisconsin."

She smiled. He *was* crazy, but if planning his move kept him happy, she'd support him all the way. "In the meantime, what are you going to do here in Chicago to drop your blood pressure?"

"Eat better, exercise, that sort of thing." He shrugged and drank some wine. "Try to relax, enjoy myself more."

"Hmm." Bridget smiled. So maybe her plan to seduce him could be thrown into that category. She finished her pasta and stood to carry her plate into the kitchen.

He jumped up and took the plate from her, his fingers covering hers before he hastily moved away. "I'll clean later."

"Sounds good," she called to his retreating back. She picked up her wineglass and carried it to sit on his big brown leather couch. She crossed her legs, letting her pump dangle from her foot. Constant walking around the city had kept her calves nice and firm.

Adam returned with a platter. "I have dessert—" He broke off when he spotted her across the room.

"Why don't we have dessert over here? More relaxing," she said, parroting his earlier words.

"Okay." He sat a safe distance away on the couch and offered her the plate of cylindrical tan pastries dusted with powdered sugar. "The house specialty is cannoli."

"I don't think I've tried cannoli before, but it looks delicious." She bit into the crisp treat. The almond-flavored filling exploded in her mouth and she moaned in delight.

"What do you think of that?" Adam's voice took on a huskier tone as he watched her.

"It's hard on the outside, but sweet and creamy on

the inside." She delicately licked a drop of cream off the corner of her mouth and watched him gulp.

She nibbled on the cannoli, locking eyes with Adam. His eyes had deepened to almost black, and his chest rose and fell rapidly. Her own breathing was just as fast.

"Would you like some?" Without waiting for an answer, she swiped a fingerful of filling off the pastry's end and brushed his firm lips, daring him to open up. He resisted for a second, his eyes boring into hers. Eventually, he opened his lips and sucked her finger inside the warm recesses of his mouth.

He swirled his tongue around her finger, just like he had teased her nipples that night in her apartment. Jolts of sensation shot up her arm and down into her unconfined breasts. They swelled, the hard tips rubbing against the soft angora. She was practically naked under her sweater.

He noticed, too. His eyes dropped from hers to her breasts. He slowly slid her finger out of his mouth, giving one last nibble with his strong white teeth.

He grabbed another pastry and ate it quickly, edging back from her. Still wary.

She tried another tack—honesty. "Adam, I know you're worried about me dancing at Frisky's."

He frowned. "I've goofed this thing up from the first. Instead of discouraging you the last time, I've been worried that my, um, eager response made you decide to try dancing for them. Why else would you be at a strip club?"

"It was for business, but not what you're imagining. I've been designing specialty lingerie and costumes for Sugar and some other dancers. Last Friday, I was delivering Sugar's new outfit."

"Sewing stripper clothes." The puzzle pieces seemed to click together in his head. "That's why you had that lime-green bra and plastic high heels at your apartment."

She put down her cannoli and touched his knee. "I should have told you from the beginning what I was doing there at Frisky's, but you laughed at the idea that I could be a dancer, and I lost my temper."

He shook his head. "I never thought you *couldn't* be a dancer—it's that I didn't think you would *want* to."

"I don't want to, but I wanted you to think of me as somebody besides your friends' little sister." She pulled back her hand and blinked. Darn it, why was this so hard? It wasn't as if she wanted to marry the guy and move to his dairy farm. She just wanted to finish what they'd started last week.

"Believe me, Bridget, that's not a problem anymore." He swiped his hand across his face. "So all that dancing you did for me—what was that?"

She took a deep breath. It was now or never. "You've kept me at arm's length for years, and now

I want to get close to you." She scooted next to him. "As close as possible."

He groaned. "You know what you're asking of me? What about your family?"

"I'm a grown woman now. What happens in Chicago, stays in Chicago."

He gave her a wry grin. "I think that's Vegas."

"Then let's go to Vegas. You should take a vacation anyway." She turned sideways on the couch, her knee touching his thigh. "We both get what we need this way. You said you wanted to relax and enjoy yourself."

"And you? What do you get, Bridget?" He touched her hand and moved his fingers to the edge of her sweater.

"I get *you*." Her boldness scared and exhilarated her. "All of you, all over me. All *in* me."

"You don't know what you're asking." He gripped her wrist. "I can't promise you anything. If you have some sugar-sweet, princess-pink idea of what it would be like—"

She interrupted him. "I know exactly what I'm asking. I want it all. I trust you."

He studied her face, his dark eyes burning into her. "It would take a stronger man than me to refuse you again."

"So don't." Her lips curved into a triumphant smile.

He lifted an eyebrow and shook his head in

amusement. "I won't." He looked at her sweater. "You spilled some powdered sugar. Let me get it for you." Still holding her wrist, he used his other hand to deliberately stroke the exposed V of skin above her neckline. He slowly moved his hand over her collarbone. She closed her eyes and shuddered as his palm brushed over first one nipple, then the other.

The soft angora tickled her bare skin, thanks to the surprise she was wearing. He massaged her breasts with both hands, the sensitized tips jutting into the soft knit.

The hidden place between her thighs throbbed and swelled, a cool current of air teasing her dampness. Leaning in, he flicked his tongue around her ear and trailed to the V of her sweater. He inhaled deeply. "Exactly like I remembered. Your skin is softer than the sweater."

Okay, that was enough foreplay. Just as she was about to topple onto the couch and demand that he hurry, he stood and walked to the iPod he had hooked into the entertainment center.

A couple pushes of the buttons and Norah Jones's sultry voice spilled from the speakers. Adam sat on the couch. "Dance for me."

"Dance?" She glanced at the empty floor space between the coffee table and the entertainment center.

"Strip for me," he clarified. "Like you did the first time. Only now we both know how the song ends."

6

So Adam thought he knew what to expect? He was in for a shock. Bridget pushed off the couch and stood in front of him. She rolled her shoulders and took a deep breath, drawing the music into her.

Swaying her hips gently, she gazed straight into his eyes. The girls at Frisky's hid themselves emotionally. But Bridget had waited too long for this moment to hide one single bit. She would put it all out there for Adam. He might not realize that, but she'd know. No more hiding.

She unzipped the side of her skirt, pushing it over her hips with a little wiggle. It fell to the floor and she stepped out of it, careful not to lift her leg too high.

Her brand-new black satin panties were like old-fashioned drawers, loose and full-cut reaching to the tops of her thigh-high stockings. She ran her hand down her hip, pretending to pull up the elastic band of one stocking.

He casually leaned on the couch, the only sign of

tension his right hand flexing. She twirled on her toes, stopping to face away from him. She peeked over her shoulder at him and pouted her lips in an air kiss, channeling her inner Marilyn Monroe.

He raised an eyebrow, and she caught a twinkle in his eye. Still with her back to him, she gripped the bottom of her sweater. Slowly, very slowly, she raised her arms until her sweater pulled free of her head. She tossed the red angora top onto a nearby chair and put her hands on her hips.

She'd bet Adam didn't look so blasé anymore. Her strapless undergarment was cut low to reveal most of her back. Bridget picked up her freshly highlighted hair and slowly shook it onto her bare shoulders. She swayed her hips in a matching shimmy.

"Turn around." His commanding tone sent a shiver through her. Mild Adam had been replaced by Wild Adam, the man she'd heard about but only briefly experienced. She crossed her arms in front of her breasts and slowly spun. Her heart was beating like crazy.

His jaw fell open and he swallowed hard. "What are you wearing?"

Her arms dropped to her sides as she followed Sugar's advice. Shoulders back and chest out. Literally. Her black corset was what she called "peek-a-boob"—the bra cups either folded up to cover the breasts or tucked down to bare them. The cups were down currently, baring her nipples and the upper curves of her breasts.

Bridget looked right into Adam's eyes. *Here I am, see me, take me.* Forget her body, her heart was barest of all.

"Adam." Her voice was a whisper compared to the music, but he acted as if she'd shouted.

"Bridget." He made as if to stand, but she shooed him back.

"Let me do this for you. And for me." Her gaze locked with his. He sat, but on the couch's edge. She walked to a nearby matching leather chair and extended one black-stockinged leg onto the arm. She ran her fingers up her foot to her knee and slowly continued on to her thigh.

Did she dare? Well, she'd come this far. She separated the fabric in her panties, showing him the wet curls and pale flesh previously hidden.

His eyes widened. "What kind of outfit is that?"

She gave him a smug look. "An old-fashioned outfit for an old-fashioned girl. A corset and drawers."

He furrowed his brow in confusion and then smiled, obviously remembering what he'd said to her. It was a wolfish smile, full of deviltry and promise. "Old-fashioned girls do as they're told."

She started to protest and subsided into an uncharacteristically meek silence. If playing Adam's game got her what she wanted, she'd go along with it. She didn't know what would happen, but this time he wasn't about to send her away. Not with that impressive arousal. "I can do whatever you want."

"Sit in the chair." He pointed to where she dangled her foot. She sat, keeping her knees incongruously together. As her breasts rose and fell in anticipation, she caught his interested eye.

"Touch your breasts."

She cupped them and circled her nipples with her fingertips.

He smiled, pleased with her compliance. "Relax your legs."

She let her knees fall to one side, knowing that wasn't what he had in mind.

He stood, shaking his head. "You old-fashioned girls don't know what a man wants, do you? That's okay. I'm a good teacher. I'll show you exactly what I like and how I like it, whenever I want it."

She nodded her head eagerly. Oh, yeah, whenever he wanted it sounded good. He squatted in front of her, a lock of black hair falling over his forehead as he gently pulled her knees apart. "There." He stared at her most private area. "Oh, I like *that*. Crotchless panties."

"Historically accurate drawers," she corrected, fighting not to cover herself modestly with her hands. Maybe she was more old-fashioned than she thought.

"I didn't get to see you so well last time." He took

one ankle and lifted her leg sideways over the chair arm and did the same with the other.

The slick leather and cool air tickled her bottom. She found herself wriggling under his gaze, embarrassed and aroused all at once.

"So pretty and pink." He slid a finger around the drawers' opening, brushing her skin with the lightest of touches. "And you were sitting across from me all evening like this and I never knew it. All I had to do was push up your skirt and sweater and you would have been naked under my hands." He sounded regretful at the time wasted dining.

She nodded, closing her eyes in anticipation as he circled closer to her clitoris. Her eyes flew open as his mouth touched her instead of his fingers. "Adam!"

He grinned up at her, his dark eyes flashing. "Naked under my mouth." He dipped down and flicked his tongue over her labia, trailing to her clitoris, where he made several circles before pressing hard. She clenched her thighs around his ears in surprise. His cheeks were smooth as satin, as if he'd shaved right before her arrival.

Pushing her legs into place, he went on with his mouth and tongue, doing all sorts of naughty stuff that she'd only read about. Her previous experiences had been sloppy and vaguely embarrassing, unlike now.

"Sweet and wet, just like I thought."

She clutched at his head, the black strands slipping through her fingers. His tangy scent, almost like pine trees after rain, rose to her hyperstimulated senses.

He slipped his hand under her bottom and tipped her even farther into his mouth. Bridget gave up all pretense of having a skeletal system and slid bonelessly down the chair, Adam the only stop between her and a Bridget-sized puddle on the floor. His mouth drove her crazy, little fronds of sensation feathering from her clitoris to branch into her belly.

He played with her bottom cheeks with his thumbs and dove his tongue deep inside her. She couldn't help it; she slung her legs off the chair and gripped his head again. The slide of his cheeks on her inner thighs was heavenly. Her gasps and groans turned into a shriek as he sucked her clitoris. Damn it, this was too fast, too hard, too much like the first time.

Adam pressed her bottom hole causing her to let loose another shriek. That was *certainly* not like the first time. But the thought flew away as her orgasm swept through her like a savage windstorm.

She wiggled and pressed her legs so hard around Adam's head she was sure she'd have permanent earmarks on her thighs. He kept on her relentlessly, extending her climax into long minutes of ecstasy.

He finally pulled away from her and undid his

shirt, almost popping buttons in his excitement. Bridget's eyes widened as his muscular chest was exposed. He was lean and strong, but not bulky. The black hair curling over his chest tapered into a narrow line disappearing below his waist.

What did he look like down there? Obviously he was big, judging from the bulge in his pants, but even with her somewhat limited experience of naked men, she knew there was quite a variety.

He tossed his shirt away and undid his belt buckle. As he shoved down his briefs, his erection sprang free. She unconsciously licked her lips. He looked delicious, long, dark and hard, capped with a wide tip that would stretch every inch of her. Her body clenched in anticipation.

Before he got his pants off, Bridget slipped off the leather chair and onto her knees. His protest trailed off into a groan as she took him into her mouth. He was smooth and silky, his hot skin almost scorching her lips. His head was firm and sleek as she ran her tongue around its girth and sucked hard, capturing his slightly salty taste.

He swayed slightly and she reached around to cup his tight butt with her hands. He wasn't going anywhere, not until she'd had her fill. He tangled his fingers in her hair but didn't push her away.

She relaxed her throat and pulled him deeper, his shaft dragging along her teeth. He didn't seem to mind though, thrusting into her mouth as she dropped her jaw farther. His musky male scent intoxicated her. She wanted him to rub it all over her naked body so she would never forget this moment.

ADAM STARED AT Bridget's rapt attention to his cock. Her eyes were closed in concentration and pleasure as she sucked him, her breasts swaying in time to his thrusts. She even gave soft hums of delight as she took him deeper.

Never in a million years had he thought that she'd do this for him. Dreamed it, yeah, sure, but not dared to even think it. He'd made a halfhearted attempt to stop her, but she'd grabbed his ass and was still kneading his muscles with her strong fingers.

Her mouth was as wet and hot as her pussy had been. Her tongue flicked over his head and he groaned again, grinding his cock deep. His whole body tightened; he was close to the edge now. "Bridget!" Her name came out harsher than he intended. She looked up at him in surprise, her big blue eyes as round as her lips around him. "Bridget," he continued, easing her away from him, "another minute and I'll embarrass myself again."

Understanding lit her face and she grinned, her mouth slick. "Why didn't you say so?" She stretched her arms above her head, brushing her breasts over his cock. His rock-hard shaft touching her nipples was too much to bear.

"Get on that chair now," he rasped. She gave him a sly look but complied. He kicked off the rest of his clothes and grabbed a condom from his wallet.

She sat demurely and spread her knees, hooking her legs over the chair's arms. Her lovely pink pussy shone at him, the blond curls darkened with her liquid desire.

Another few seconds and he'd be there, inside her. Finally. He fumbled the condom but managed to don it with shaking hands.

He stalked toward her. "Touch yourself. I want you to come again with me, and I can't wait any longer."

Her eyes widened but she slid a hand to her tiny button and stroked it. She let out a moan and bit her plump red bottom lip. Her other hand went to her even plumper breast, teasing her nipple into a gumdrop-sized treat for him to suck.

He bent forward, disguising the fact that his legs had actually weakened as he gazed at her lush pink-and-white beauty, highlighted by the wicked black lingerie. If the panties hadn't been crotchless, he would have ripped the seam open with his teeth to get to her.

"Ready?" he managed to ask before prodding her

slick passage. His head went in, her grip so tight they both gasped. He checked to make sure she was okay, and a stunning thought hit him.

"Sweetheart, you've done this before, right? I mean, I'm not the first…"

She laughed. "No. But it's been a while." She locked her legs around his waist and pulled him in all the way.

His eyes almost rolled up in his head as her hot, wet depths threatened his tenuous control. It had been a long time for him, too. He eased out reluctantly and immediately thrust in. Her lush mouth made a little "oh" of surprise and her muscles tightened around him.

He stared into her bright eyes. "Bridget…" He trailed off, words failing him. How could he describe the amazing rightness of holding her, of being tucked tight in her pliant body? It was as if he'd waited for her forever.

He brought himself back to the moment. It was just the newness of being with her, nothing more. His toes dug into the rug and he thrust into her again. Her stockinged legs were silky smooth against his hips, but nothing was as silky as her flesh surrounding his cock.

For one crazy minute, he wished he hadn't used a condom, wanted her hot moisture bathing his cock. Even through the thin latex, he could tell she was soaking wet. Maybe further into their relationship, if she used another kind of protection…

Relationship? He pulled up short at that line of thought when she slipped a finger between their bodies and caressed her clit.

Her finger tickled the top of his penis, shy at first, but then faster and more daring as her desire rebuilt to match his.

He sped his thrusts, dying a bit every time he withdrew and moaning with relief on reentry. Bridget tipped her head, an orgasmic blush blooming from her breasts and throat into her cheeks.

He licked her earlobe. "Come on, Bridget, come for me, you bad girl," he whispered, releasing the frantic emotions churning through his mind. "Your nipples and your pussy bare under your clothes, you letting me fuck you in a chair."

She froze, and he thought he'd gone too far talking dirty to her. But her pause was just like the roller-coaster car sitting at the top of the track before she fell into a cock-wrenching climax, clawing his back and almost knocking him off balance with her wild hip thrusts. He held on tight, desperate to catch every last squeeze before he lost control.

"Oh, Adam…yesss." Her little breathy moan, full of wonder and pure fulfillment, sent him plunging after her in his own orgasm. He twisted into her so hard and fast, he thought the condom would break as he spent himself until he was empty.

Only the shaking of his leg muscles brought him back from that delicious place between her thighs. He withdrew carefully and stepped back, his head bowed as he caught his breath.

How long had it been for him since he'd had sex like that? He shook his head. Never, if he were honest. And whatever noble intentions he'd had previously about easing away from her had disappeared in an orgasmic fog. He'd pleasure her as often and as much as she wanted, as long as she realized he wasn't a forever kind of guy.

He had no business even pretending otherwise. A girl like Bridget deserved somebody who had a real family, who knew what a normal life was all about.

"Adam?" He raised his head at her sweetly hesitant voice.

"What, sweetheart?" Her glistening pink flesh distracted him. He bet she would be ready again in no time with just a few licks—he wondered if she'd be too shy to sit on his face, or—

"Adam," she repeated, interrupting his reverie.

He dragged his glance to her face. She bit her lip. "About what you said, right before I, uh…"

"I'm sorry, Bridget. I got a little raw there. If you don't like it, I won't do it." That would be difficult to remember, though, considering how she'd responded to him.

"No—you surprised me because I've never had

anyone say stuff like that before." She took a deep breath as if confessing a dark secret. "I did like it."

So his old-fashioned Bridget had a naughty side. If he hadn't already seen her lingerie, her incredible response to his words confirmed it.

A smile of anticipation curved his mouth. He'd told her he liked it with an edge sometimes, and maybe she'd like to try those things with him.

But not on that chair again. His legs were killing him. "Honestly, Bridget, for once I want to be with you on something besides living-room furniture. Between your futon and my chair, we haven't had the chance to get horizontal." He stood and tugged her from the chair.

She smiled coyly. "Is it my fault you can't wait long enough to get to the bedroom?"

"Yes." He gave her a scorching kiss. "Yes, it is most definitely your fault." He swung her into his arms and strode to his bedroom, Bridget giggling wildly all the way. "But you can make it up to me in my big, comfortable bed. Several times might do it, but I wouldn't count on it."

7

"BRIDGET. BRIDGET, wake up." Adam's voice teased at her ear. Even on a Sunday, he woke early. This Sunday, he'd reached for her in the predawn darkness and made love to her until she'd fallen asleep in exhaustion.

She groaned and rolled over in his bed, pulling the covers high over her naked body. If it was before ten, she wasn't moving.

He drew back a corner of the brick-red duvet. "I have coffee."

Rats. He did have coffee. Really good-smelling coffee, like maybe it had vanilla or hazelnut in it. But to drink it, she'd have to uncover her head. And she knew her haircut that looked fun and sexy after proper styling became a major case of bedhead in the morning.

In the couple of weeks she and Adam had been sleeping together, she had either managed to get into the shower while he was out of the room or had slipped on a headband or scrunchie stashed in the nightstand.

"Coffee's getting cold." He sounded amused. "Come out, come out, wherever you are."

"Fine." She emerged from the bedding like a turtle sticking its head out from its shell, resisting the urge to finger-comb her hair. After all, they'd made themselves plenty familiar with every inch of each other's bodies—what was a little bedhead between lovers?

Apparently not just a little bedhead, judging from his wide eyes and hastily suppressed grin. He immediately tried to cover it by quickly handing the coffee to her.

"Thanks." She tucked the sheet around her breasts and accepted the white mug with the red-and-black UW-Madison badger mascot on it. Seeing it reminded her of how she'd seen the sights of Madison, Wisconsin, but not Chicago, her home for the last seven months. Unless seeing Adam, one of the wonders of Chicago, counted. "Let's go do the tourist thing today, Adam."

"Tourist thing?" He sat on the bed's edge facing her, his broad shoulders outlined in a lightweight knit sweater. The olive-green shade played up his black hair and dark brown eyes. And how on earth did Adam always look tanned, even at the end of a long winter? It must be from some Mediterranean ancestor, since she could testify in a court of law that he had no tanning booth lines anywhere on his body.

She sipped the coffee, sighing in satisfaction as the tasty brew slipped down her throat. "Yeah, I'd like to see the sights. Between school and work, I haven't seen anything of the city."

He looked thoughtful. "Let me grab the events calendar from the *Trib* and see what's on today. It seems like pretty good weather for late March." He grinned. "Love the hair."

"Oh, you…" She grabbed a pillow and tossed it at him. He ducked easily, his eyes flashing in laughter. "Get that newspaper and stop teasing me."

"You want teasing, I'll show you teasing." He plucked the mug from her hand and set it on the cherrywood nightstand. Amidst her squeals of mock protest, he flicked the duvet down to the foot of the sleigh bed and covered her breast with his hand.

Bridget slumped against the headboard as he caressed her. She reached for him, but he dropped a kiss on her breast and stood. "Now that's teasing."

"No, *this* is teasing." She deliberately spread her legs and stroked her clit a half-dozen times. "Oops, I think my coffee's getting cold." She stopped and reached for her mug and drank deeply. "Delicious."

The stunned look on his face was worth the unsatisfied pulse thrumming through her lower body. Just as he was about to kiss her, his cell phone on the nightstand rang. He pulled back slightly. "Let me forward this to voice mail·and we'll continue where we left off."

He looked at the caller ID display and fumbled

the phone, almost dropping it in his haste to stop the ringing.

"Who was it?"

He was wearing a peculiar look of distaste or disgust. "Nobody," he said, so forcefully that his voice echoed through the quiet bedroom.

"Oh-kay." None of her business.

"No, I'm sorry." He sighed. "An ex-girlfriend. We ended it months ago and I haven't talked to her since."

"Rough breakup, huh?" That girlfriend must have been colossally stupid to let Adam get away. *Isn't that what you'll be once you've gotten him out of your system and break up?* She scowled at that too darn perceptive little voice in her head.

Adam must have mistaken her uncomfortable introspection for disgruntlement because he hastily went on reassure her, "I would have told you, but she is so completely gone, I never thought to mention her. She probably just wants to borrow money, anyway."

"Tell her to get a job." Bridget had no sympathy for people who didn't get off their duffs and do something.

He finally laughed. "If I have the bad misfortune to run in to her again, I'll tell her."

"You do that." She smiled at him and tried to pull him into bed.

He pulled away. "Sorry, honey. That phone call

pretty much wrecked the mood." He kissed the top of her head. "Maybe later, huh?"

"Sure." She watched him leave the room. It was the first time he'd passed on sex. That stupid ex-girl-friend had really done a number on him.

Bridget called down the hall that she was hopping into the shower. During her quick shampoo and hair-styling, she fretted about the phone call. Did he still have feelings for his ex? According to Bridget's brothers, Adam was a sucker for sob stories when it came to people he cared about, or at least felt an ob-ligation to. Like his parents, whom he'd bailed out of several insanely stupid situations.

Her brave knight on a white horse. But if the ex thought she'd get another ride with Adam, Bridget would just have to knock her off and toss her under the hooves.

"HOLY COW, IT'S HOT IN HERE." Bridget opened her goose-down jacket and wiped a bead of sweat off her forehead. Late March in Chicago was a bit warmer than Wisconsin, but still below freezing.

"Nice and steamy." Adam winked at her. She was glad to see him getting back to his usual self. "You've been saying how you haven't seen any green growing things lately, so I thought you'd enjoy the Lincoln Park tropical plant conservatory."

"It's wonderful." She tied her jacket around her

waist and wandered down the narrow bark-paved path before stopping to look at a delicate pink orchid. "Someday I'd like to have a greenhouse and grow these."

"You can take the girl out of the farm but you can't take the farm out of the girl."

She shrugged. "I do miss the flowers. I haven't seen anything green since last September." Between the gray city landscape and her busy schedule, she hadn't visited any of the indoor gardens dotting the city. After all, according to the sign at the conservatory entrance, Chicago's motto was *Urbs in Horto,* or City in a Garden.

"That's right—all those flower gardens on the farm were yours, weren't they?"

"It's one thing I do miss about the farm." She had a few houseplants in her apartment but they were looking pretty sad these days.

"And you always left room for your mom's tomato and pepper plants. Remember on my visit there when you planted the moonlight garden?"

"It was in the best light and closest to the back door so I could step outside in the evening and enjoy the fragrance of the flowers."

He pointed to a white orchid. "Maybe you could grow one of those."

She spotted the plant's information tag. "I doubt it. According to this, *angraecum sesquipedale* is the rarest of all orchids from Madagascar, only growing in the eastern rain forests. I've never grown anything that difficult before."

"I think you could if you wanted to. After all, how many stripper outfits did you sew before you left Wisconsin?"

She looked around to make sure no one was near enough to hear his teasing and made as if to punch him in the bicep.

He caught her hand easily and kissed her knuckles. "What I meant was, you can do anything you set your mind to."

"Well, thank you." A warm feeling that had nothing to do with the steamy greenhouse spread through her.

He smiled at her and tucked her hand into the bend of his elbow. "You're welcome." As they strolled deeper into the jungle, he cleared his throat. "Bridget, I always wondered. Why did your brothers go off to UW-Madison right after high school, but you stayed at home and went to community college? You must have had the grades to get into a four-year school."

Bridget immediately tensed. Adam noticed how her fingers dug into his arm and raised an eyebrow. "Touchy subject?"

She deliberately eased her grip on him. "Right after high school, I actually got accepted to the school I'm currently attending."

"Here? In Chicago?" He gave her a puzzled look. "Why did you wait six years?"

She purposely deepened her voice. "'If you think Bob and Helen Weiss are going to let their little girl move to the big, bad city, you've got another think coming.'" She grimaced. "That was pretty much our discussion back then."

"They didn't want you to go to college?" He stopped in the middle of the path, his indignation cheering her unhappy memories.

"The farm was having some financial trouble and they couldn't afford to help with tuition, especially since my design school is a private college. So I decided that if I were going to pay for my own education, it would be at my first choice of schools. It took six years to save the money but I eventually made it here. I sewed prom dresses, clerked at the feed store and sold boxed bras and panty packs at the discount store."

"Good for you, Bridget."

She tugged him along to look at a lacy golden orchid. "When I told my parents last spring that I was moving to Chicago they weren't happy, but Colin and Dane assured them you'd keep an eye on me."

He squirmed a bit. "You haven't told them about us, have you?"

"No, what's to tell? They wouldn't understand our no-strings relationship, anyway." Despite their own randy pasts, her brothers expected her to marry as a virgin and only have sex for the purpose of having kids. Certainly not for fun.

He relaxed. "I didn't figure you had. Especially since your brothers haven't shown up to put their fists in my face."

She made a dismissive motion with her free hand. "You and I both know what those clowns have gotten themselves into over the years."

"Yeah, but it's different for guys."

"Tell me about it." She didn't bother to hide her sour tone. Part of the reason her parents had been too strapped to help her with school was because of the loans they signed for her brothers' educations. The boys were supposed to pay them back after graduation, but Colin had gotten married right out of college and Dane had gone on to grad school and hadn't earned any money for a couple more years. Whatever financial arrangements they had made since then were strictly between them.

"Are they helping you this year?"

"No, and frankly I wouldn't let them even if they offered. First, my parents need to save money for retirement and second, I don't want any obligations to study what they think I should be studying."

"My parents probably would have helped me through college if I'd majored in agronomy."

"Really? Crops and plant science?" She wrinkled

her nose. Adam's parents had never taken an interest in his education. "Why agronomy?"

He winked at her. "So I could grow bigger and better pot plants for them." According to Adam, his parents had been dedicated stoners. Surely they'd outgrown that now that they were in their fifties.

She snorted. "Just think—a new elective for the ag college. 'Methods of Marijuana Enhancement and Cultivation'."

"Standing room only." He nodded in mock seriousness.

She snickered. "Except everyone would keep falling over."

"Or leaving to get snacks from the vending machine," he continued.

Bridget spotted a tall, spiky-leafed plant that resembled marijuana and pointed it out to him. They clutched at each other and laughed themselves silly in the middle of the conservatory. Several other visitors passed them, some with exasperated looks and others with amused, tolerant expressions as if remembering their own youthful infatuations.

She impulsively stood on tiptoe and planted a kiss on his cheek. "Thanks. I was starting to wallow in self-pity there for a moment."

He brought their still-entwined hands to his lips and again kissed her knuckles. "You wouldn't have wallowed for long. That's what I like about you,

Bridget. You have a great go-get-'em attitude. Look at how you went after me."

"And are you glad I did?" She gave him a satisfied smile.

"Hmm." He frowned in puzzlement as if seriously considering his answer. "I think I am, yes."

"You *think* you are?" She pushed him past the faux marijuana plant and through the conservatory exit. "Why don't you think about it while we eat? I have the munchies now."

JUST WHAT BRIDGET had been dying to see on her tour of Chicago—the backside of a cow. *Not.* The cow in question shifted her weight from hoof to hoof, obviously used to being on public display in the small Lincoln Park zoo.

But Adam watched in fascination as the blond-ponytailed zookeeper gave the basics of how to milk a cow. Bridget tried not to yawn. The keeper obviously knew what she was doing as she hooked the cow to the zoo's slightly older-model milking machine, but she wasn't explaining every single step to the audience, thereby making it look a lot easier than it actually was.

Bridget's gaze idly traced the complex tubing and pipes needed for comfortable, effective milking and noted the vacuum gauge was creeping higher. They needed to adjust the suction so they didn't injure the teats.

But all Adam and the audience saw was the udder-fresh milk gushing into the long hose and traveling into the milk line.

He nudged her with his elbow. "Isn't this neat? Just clean the udder, hook them up and watch the milk go."

"Um, Adam, there's a lot more to this…." She stopped after seeing his shining eyes.

The keeper was telling a story about a city power outage over the summer that had knocked out their electric-powered milking machines. "So we called in all the keepers and anyone who knew their way around a cow so we could hand-milk the herd."

Bridget winced in sympathy. Hand-milking even a small herd like the zoo's was a good way to give yourself carpal tunnel syndrome, not to mention what it did to your back crouching down to an udder. Maybe she should volunteer to be a zoo emergency cow-milker, like a dairy paramedic. She could sew herself a superhero costume—maybe some black-and-white-spotted Holstein cotton print.

The zookeeper finished her presentation, much to Adam's disappointment. "I wanted to hear more." He looked around the barn. "Do they give continuing ed classes on it?"

Poor guy, he was so earnest, Bridget couldn't help but smile. He was going after his dairy farm goal with the single-mindedness that he used for everything else. "Come here." She grabbed his elbow and pointed out several milking machine features that the keeper had omitted.

With his quick mind, he learned the basic engineering behind the vacuums and pumps. "And during the blackout, why didn't they just let the cows wait until the power came on?"

Wow. He also needed to take Remedial Bovine Physiology 101. Anyone who'd even been near a cow would know the answer to that. "Even a couple hours matters since the cows can't turn the milk on and off like a faucet. If they don't get milked, their udders can swell like balloons and get infected. Believe me, you don't want a whole herd with mastitis."

"Oh."

"Don't worry." She patted his hand. "Once you quit your trading job, you can apprentice with my father or Colin and they'll teach you all you need to know."

"Thanks." His grateful smile quickly turned solemn. Bridget lost her smile as well, the pleasures of their day together dimming a bit. Adam the Wisconsin dairy farmer would be just as far from her reach as Adam the Chicago futures trader once was.

"DO YOU HAVE A MINUTE before your next class, Bridget?"

Bridget looked up from packing her books and

sketches. Jennifer Miller, her apparel-construction instructor, stood next to her. "Sure, this is my last class today." She was stopping at Frisky's after school to drop off an order for Sugar. Was she in trouble? She always turned in all her assignments.

"Mine, too." Jennifer ran a hand through her short black hair. As befitting her job, her white blouse and charcoal-gray pants .were perfectly tailored to fit her tiny frame. She wore a red-and-black necklace of chunky Bakelite beads that resembled some of Bridget's grandmother's jewelry. "Your latest project was. very well done. I especially enjoyed how you built such a supportive bra into that spaghetti-strap camisole."

"Thank you." Bridget smiled in relief and gestured to her own body, today fortunately clad in a stylish pale-green pencil skirt with a bust-minimizing pink wrap blouse. Since her makeover, she'd practiced her sewing skills on clothes for herself. "As you can see, I like to design undergarments for women like me who can't just slip on a skimpy top and cross their fingers that everything stays put."

Jennifer laughed. "Everything of mine stays put more than I'd like. But as you know, the majority of American women are size fourteen and larger, so this type of design has a real market."

"Of course." Bridget reached for her sketchbook and flipped open to the drawing of her black lace bra and matching thong. "I designed this for myself. And for a friend," she added, remembering the ivory version she'd done for Sugar.

Jennifer stared at the sketch, her expression hard to read. "And you put it together, sewed it yourself?"

"Yes, and it's quite comfortable—no neck or shoulder aches even after a long day." She looked in her bag and spotted the pale pink bra on its way to Sugar. "I have one that I'm delivering to my client tonight." Bridget pulled out the bra and unwrapped the tissue paper around it.

"May I?" Bridget nodded and Jennifer took the bra by the straps. Her eyes widened as the large cups unfolded. "What size does your client wear?"

"Thirty-six G."

Jennifer examined the bra closely. Bridget hoped she'd clipped all the stray threads and hadn't missed any raw fabric edges. She looked at Bridget. "Nicely sewn, but what does your client think?"

"This is the fourth one she's ordered in this style, and she says it's the only style that doesn't cut into her shoulders or make her back sore. I've also sewn other outfits for her and her friends."

"Very good." Her teacher smiled. "Is your client a performer, by any chance?"

Bridget blinked in surprise. "Well, yes, she's a dancer at a club nearby. How did you guess?"

"Most women this size have implants, and I

noticed a sketch for an exotic dancer costume in your papers while you were handing in your last assignment."

"Oh." Bridget mentally cursed herself for being careless with her designs. How was she supposed to be taken seriously if word got around that she sewed striptease outfits?

Jennifer held up her hand. "Don't worry. I started out designing costumes for female impersonators, which taught me more than I learned in my first couple years in fashion-design school. If you can support a pair of G-cup breasts comfortably or disguise a grown man's package in a tight satin evening gown, you're off to a good start."

Bridget returned her instructor's smile. "Thanks."

Jennifer became all business. "Okay, now that I know this, I definitely think you should enter an upcoming lingerie design contest. I don't usually recommend first-year students, but you have a lot of experience and your dancer clients wouldn't keep you on if they didn't like your work."

"That's for sure." If the costume didn't make money, it was gone.

"The contest deadline is in two weeks." Jennifer walked over to her desk and opened a manila folder. "Here's the entry form." She handed the package to Bridget, who read the fancy script at the top.

"It's sponsored by Richard's on Rodeo?"

Jennifer smiled. "Actually, it's pronounced Ree-shard's on Ro-day-o. Its flagship lingerie boutique is on Rodeo Drive in Beverly Hills with several smaller locations throughout Southern California."

Bridget blushed at her mispronunciation. "Beverly Hills? That's too fancy for my designs. I only have big bras and stripper clothes in my portfolio right now."

Her teacher threw back her head and laughed. "Bridget, have you ever been to Southern California?"

She shook her head, and Jennifer continued, "A lot of women there have implants—small bands and big cups. Also, what you call stripper clothes are very popular among the young, rich set. Just upgrade the fabrics and trims and you're good to go."

She must have still looked skeptical because Jennifer planted her hand on the desk. "Trust me— I've been in this business forever and I have an eye for it. Just do it. You won't be sorry."

Her teacher's conviction strengthened her resolve. She hadn't come to Chicago to let life pass her by. "Okay, I'll do it."

"Good. Since I have to sign off on your papers, I'll need your completed application package one week from today, samples and all."

Bridget gulped. One week? That didn't give her any time to draw new designs. She'd be pushing it to get her samples finished.

Jennifer pointed to the smaller print on the application. "First prize is ten thousand dollars and a design contract with Richard."

Bridget's jaw dropped. For ten thousand bucks and a design contract, she'd sew a bra and panties for Ree-shard himself.

"DARIA? WHAT ARE you doing here?" The girl of Adam's nightmares was standing in his office doorway. Unfortunately, Daria took his exclamation of horror as an invitation to enter.

"Adam, darling! It's so good to see you." She swooped in on him, blood-red lips puckered, but he ducked away. Still, her cloud of noxious perfume rolled over him like exhaust from a city bus. Her long brunette hair was perfectly styled and she wore a fur coat over a low-cut red dress. Fortunately for her, it was a different coat than the last time he'd seen her, otherwise he'd have thrown her straight out of his office.

"Daria, we split in November. It's almost April."

She pouted. "And it was so cruel of you to end our relationship—right before the holiest season of the year."

He shot her a skeptical look. Despite her traditional Polish upbringing, Daria was anything but religious. She probably just regretted not getting a Christmas gift from him. He decided to needle her a bit. "Don't worry, the jeweler was able to take the ring back."

That was an ill-thought bit of revenge. Her stunned expression turned greedy and made him wish he hadn't said anything.

"You bought me a ring?" she breathed. "An... engagement ring?"

What a dumb-ass he was. Dangling diamonds in front of a gold digger—even fictitious diamonds—was *not* the best way to make her leave him alone. "No! Hell, no! I bought you a sweater. I gave it to the Goodwill thrift store."

Her brow furrowed. "But, Adam, you didn't give the ring to Goodwill, did you? They do not know what to do with such nice jewelry."

"No, Daria, there was no ring. I never planned to buy you one."

"Why? Am I not beautiful enough for you?" She slowly twirled, arms outstretched.

Well, no, she wasn't. After being with Bridget, Daria's skinny body and petulant expression were no turn-on. And of course, Bridget had that inner beauty that shone from her, almost like a glow. He'd always dismissed the whole "inner beauty" thing as a scam to fix him up on a blind date with an unattractive girl, but Bridget disproved that theory.

"Adam! Adam!" Daria's nagging voice dragged him back to reality. "Aren't I *gorgeous?*"

He wiped the goofy grin off his face that appeared more and more when he thought of Bridget. Despite their unpleasant past, he wasn't cruel enough to deliberately crush Daria's fragile ego. He prevaricated, "Many men would find you attractive."

That was true. Bridget's brother Dane had nearly tripped over his tongue when they dropped him off after Bridget's move last fall. Though Daria had opened her mouth to tear a strip off him for being five minutes late and totally ruined Dane's fantasy.

"Oh, Adam," Daria cooed. "Why don't we try again?" She tried to wrap her arms around his neck, but he disentangled himself from her grasp.

"Try again? Are you joking?" Enough was enough. "While we were dating you were meeting sugar daddies on your modeling trips." He gestured at her coat, total overkill on a nice spring day. "Which sucker bought you that?"

She actually tried to remember for a second and rallied. "But all of that doesn't matter. I was simply a bit short on money, and you had all of your money in the stock market and wouldn't sell—"

What was he, an ATM? Bridget was the only one who'd point-blank refused any financial help, and she was the one he wanted to help most. His temper snapped. "You were my girlfriend, not my paid escort. Unfortunately I never realized you didn't know the difference."

"Adam!" she gasped. He grabbed her elbow to show her out but she dug in her spiked heels and pointed to his credenza. "Is that why you don't want me? That fat blonde?"

His gaze followed her pointing finger to see an older picture of him and Bridget at Colin's wedding. He'd found it at home and brought it into work. Not that he needed any excuse to moon over her. "Bridget's none of your business, so get out."

"Ha! She looks like a plump little milkmaid."

Adam whooped with ironic laughter at her uncanny guess and shoved her into the hall. "You're actually right, for once."

Daria looked down her nose. "When you get tired of bouncing around on her, call me." She stalked off on her stilettos, drawing a very interested stare from his colleague Tom, who'd been lurking near his office door.

Adam sighed and returned to the chair behind his desk. Tom crossed his arms over his chest and leaned on the doorframe. "The infamous Daria, huh? She is one hot chick. Mind passing me her number?"

"You don't have enough money for her. Almost nobody does." He sure hadn't, so she must have kept him around just for sexual reasons. He grimaced. An unwitting boy toy. Maybe it was payback for his casual, sometimes careless attitude toward women in his younger years.

"Humph. My ex-wife has all my money, but maybe I can fake it for a while." He gave Adam a hopeful grin.

"Stick with strippers, Tom. They're more honest than Daria."

"Speaking of strippers, did you ever find that girl at Frisky's? I gotta admit, you were the last guy I expected to get thrown out of a strip club." Tom laughed. "I mean, come on. You gotta misbehave pretty badly to do that."

Adam forced a chuckle. Crap. He thought Tom had been too drunk to remember any of that. "Guess all those girls went to my head. A guy has to cut loose once in a while, you know."

Tom chuckled along with him and then winced, patting his chest. "Stupid angina." He popped a tablet into his mouth.

"Geez, buddy, you have heart problems now?" Tom was only in his early forties.

He shrugged and gestured at the office. "Everybody here over forty does, Hale. Trading's a young guy's game. Sooner or later your doc will yap at you about your blood pressure, then they'll put you on some useless medication and tell you to lower your stress." He snorted.

"Why are you still here, since it's so bad for your health?"

Tom winked. "I have plans. Another couple

years and I'll have enough to retire on, so I figure these nitro pills will more than pay for themselves."

"That's risky, don't you think?"

His coworker shrugged. "We deal in risk all the time, Hale."

"Yeah, but that's different. Your health versus your money sounds like a damn poor trade-off."

"What good is health if you don't have the money to enjoy it?" Tom shrugged his shoulders. "Now unless you're going to give me Daria's number, I need to get back there and add to my retirement plan."

Adam shook his head. "It's for your own good." Not that Tom was overly concerned with his own good. "Daria's nothing but bad news," he warned him before closing his office door.

At his desk he leaned back in his chair and laced his fingers behind his head to contemplate his lucky escape. Because of Daria's modeling trip/ booty call schedule, he hadn't slept with her for several weeks before their breakup. By the time, Bridget had done her striptease for him, he'd been celibate for almost five months.

Now he couldn't be celibate for five hours without craving his plump little blond milkmaid. He checked the clock on his computer—she'd be between classes now, so he dialed her cell.

"Hi, honey." Her voice was husky and sweet. "Sell

many cows today?" That was their in-joke about his job. Her family raised cows, and he sold them.

"A whole herd. Do you have any plans for dinner?"

"What did you have in mind?"

"Steak?" he teased, her peals of laughter warming him. "Actually, I had *you* in mind for dinner."

"Me?" Her giggles turned breathless.

"Yeah." He shifted in his chair, the image of her spread under him like a pink-and-white bonbon making him hard. "For the appetizer, a nibble of your sweet lips. For the main course, your delectable breasts. And to drink, the finest of juices in a delicate pink cup, waiting to be sipped and never running dry."

"Oh, Adam." He actually heard her gulp through the phone. "I have a test in three minutes. If I flunk, it's all your fault."

"Sorry, baby, I'll make it up to you later. Be at my place at six, and bring your appetite."

"I have to stop at Frisky's, so it'll be closer to seven." She made a noise of frustration and hung up. He laughed. Her appetite was as voracious as his own, and he was beginning to think they'd never tire of each other.

ADAM PULLED the sheet to his waist and slumped onto his pillow. "Geez, I better buy some more minutes on my calling plan now that I know a quick naughty phone call can get you so revved up."

Bridget stretched next to him and smiled like the cat that ate the canary. An evening with Adam was the perfect end to a great day. "You're lucky I did okay on my test. Otherwise, there would have been no nibbling my lips, sipping cups or anything else tonight."

He yawned. "I knew you'd do fine on that test. You always were the smartest one around. Probably got your brothers' share of brains."

"If only I can borrow their luck for that contest I told you about over dinner." She'd never won a contest before except when she'd helped her mom can some blue-ribbon pickles for the county fair.

"Yeah, that's great, sweetheart. I never realized how complicated bra designs are. You have a real gift for this."

"Thank you, Adam. I appreciate that." He finally understood more about her chosen career. She rolled over to play with his chest hair. "Speaking of bras, I forgot to tell you that Sugar invited us to a party at her new condo Saturday."

"Oh, yeah?" His voice was sleepy and relaxed.

Bridget knew from experience he'd sock out in the next five minutes so she hurried on. "It's her house-warming party. Do you want to come with me?"

"If you're okay with me going. I did see her naked at Frisky's that once."

She shrugged. "Most of the men in Chicago have seen Sugar naked. Unless you're going to dump me for her, I don't care." Despite her new look, insecurity still bothered her occasionally.

He tipped her chin up and frowned at her. "If you think I'd be so shallow to do that, you're crazy. I'm sure Sugar is a fine person, but she's not you."

Bridget swallowed a lump in her throat and smiled at him. "Thank you."

"Don't thank me for telling the truth." Their tender kiss was interrupted by his massive yawn. "Sorry, baby. You just wore me out."

"Same here." She shifted onto her side and snuggled into him so that they were like spoons in a drawer.

He caressed her hip and bottom. "Sleep tight."

Bridget smiled and looked at the tiny pink mark on her breast that his lips had left. His raw passion thrilled her after all his years of restraint around her.

His breathing evened as he quickly moved into sleep, but Bridget couldn't follow him. Too many thoughts buzzing through her head like bees in her flower garden.

Where were she and Adam going? She had been content to let their relationship float along without thinking too much about the future.

She frowned over her shoulder. Why didn't he snore like her dad? Or belch the alphabet like Colin? Or have all sorts of other gross personal habits that had become old hat to her thanks to her dad, brothers and previous boyfriends?

No, Adam was perfect. She quickly amended the thought. Not perfect, she knew that. But perfect for her?

Geez. Much more of this so-called perfection and she'd be back in rural Wisconsin where she started. Adam would be the proud owner of a Wisconsin farm, like he'd always wanted, and she'd be sewing prom dresses for local teenagers at her Ping-Pong table in the evenings, like she had always *not* wanted.

But what about the nights? The nights would be like this one, his strong body and awesome mouth driving her into a frenzy before his sleep-heavy arm held her tight.

She would have to be careful for now. Because, sooner or later, things would fizzle like they had with her prior boyfriends. They could have a graceful parting, stay friends and still be cordial at family events.

Right, that hidden voice scoffed. *And when Adam and his wife invite you to their baby's christening, you'll be just fine. Maybe even sew the baby's gown.*

Ugh. No, she wouldn't be fine. She closed her eyes tightly, cows and prom dresses and christening gowns dancing through her mind until she fell asleep.

8

"Aren't you going to be chilly at your friend's party?" Adam paced across Bridget's tiny living room and frowned at her royal-blue silk halter dress for the third time. The halter fastened behind her neck and was completely backless before flaring into a full skirt. She had taken the idea from Marilyn Monroe's famous white dress in *The Seven Year Itch*.

Bridget actually enjoyed her body now. Instead of hiding it in loose clothing, she had either bought or sewn a number of classy, sexy, flattering outfits to showcase her curves.

"What do you suggest?" She had no intention of changing, but was curious what he might think of.

"Oh, I don't know. Maybe a sweater and some pants."

She scoffed. "Like my red angora sweater?" He loved it when she wore that and nothing else. Adam's obvious appreciation for her physical appearance had boosted her confidence, as well. No more apologizing for her full breasts and round butt.

"No!" The tips of his ears turned pink. "Something baggy."

"Something frumpy?" She laughed. "Come on, we're going to be late." As if she'd wear something baggy to a party full of exotic dancers who trusted her fashion and design sense.

He grumped but helped her on with her black velvet wrap.

"Don't worry, sweetie." She pinched his butt and grinned when he jumped. "I have a nice surprise for you later."

He immediately cheered up. "Here, or at my place?"

She had left so many personal things at his house that they were practically living together. She used her place mostly for working and seeing clients.

She arched an eyebrow. "Maybe neither."

His eyes widened and he yanked open her door. "Let's get to that party so we can have one of our own."

She chuckled and took his arm. Downstairs their cab was waiting for them. They held hands all the way to Sugar's condo, gossiping about work and school. Bridget rested her head on his shoulder at one point, supremely content to sit with him in silence. He smiled at her and kissed her forehead.

The cab stopped in front of Sugar's condo building, a converted warehouse in the trendy River North neighborhood. Bridget had window-shopped in its large art gallery district known as SuHu, near the intersection of Superior and Huron Streets, but had not seen the area after dark.

Club-goers in slinky, sequined clothes strolled by. Adam nodded in their direction. "Probably heading to Excalibur or another big club. We're a few blocks away. Have you ever been there?"

"No, I haven't." Frisky's had actually been the only club she'd visited while living in Chicago, but she didn't think that counted.

"Excalibur is huge and noisy, not the most romantic place around. I'll take you to a smaller place where we can actually sit and talk." He dipped his hand to the curve of her hip. "I've heard one place has booths where you can draw the curtains for total privacy."

She shivered. To have Adam touch her in public, with strangers a few feet away. Would she dare, knowing how unrestrained her response was to him?

A few minutes later, the doorman had let them in and they were ringing Sugar's doorbell on the third floor.

"Welcome." Dressed in a beautiful low-cut white silk pantsuit, Sugar threw her arms around Bridget in an enthusiastic hug. Sugar kissed Adam's cheek in greeting and hooked her arms through theirs. "Come see my new place."

Sugar left their coats in the guest bedroom and

gave them the grand tour, pointing out the hardwood floors and eleven-foot-high ceilings. She had a terrific balcony overlooking a grassy courtyard, and the lights from nearby high-rises twinkled down at them.

As Sugar left them to greet more guests, Bridget spotted Electra and Jinx and tugged Adam along to say hello. He hid a wince as Electra slapped him on the shoulder and carefully kept his gaze from dropping to where Jinx's diamond nipple jewelry pressed against her sheer black blouse.

Bridget took pity on him and asked him to get her a drink from the fully staffed bar. He escaped with an air of relief.

"What a stuffed shirt." Jinx shook her head.

"Shut up," Electra told her without heat. "He treats Bridget like a princess, and that counts for plenty in my book."

"Thanks, Electra." Bridget patted her hand. She winked at Jinx. "And he is definitely *not* a stuffed shirt."

Intrigued, Jinx badgered her for details, but Bridget only laughed.

Adam returned with champagne for her and a Guinness for himself. Jinx eyed him up and down, making him nervous until Bridget pulled him away. "Behave yourself, Jinx the Minx."

Bridget and Adam mingled among Sugar's other guests. They were an eclectic bunch, ranging from her new neighbors to business associates to fellow exotic dancers. Bridget concentrated on this last bunch, discussing costume and lingerie design. A few requested business cards, which she'd tucked into her matching blue silk purse.

Adam was a great sport while she networked, focusing on her conversations and never fidgeting or acting bored. As they left the last group she'd been talking with, she squeezed his arm. "Thank you."

He gave her a puzzled look. "You're welcome, but what for?"

"For coming along and supporting me, of course."

"I'm glad to help your career however I can. Your designs drive men crazy, as I can personally attest to." He gave her a quick kiss. "Now, how about some food?"

Just then her elegantly clad midsection gave a decidedly inelegant growl. "Good idea."

They turned the corner into the dining room where caterers were fussing over a lavish buffet. Bridget helped herself to exotic treats—crab puffs, coconut shrimp and skewered chicken satay with peanut sauce. No cocktail wienies or meatballs in grape jelly sauce here.

Adam had filled his plate with similar goodies and two plump chocolate-dipped strawberries. "For later." He winked at her.

They found space in a plush love seat tucked into a corner. Bridget set her plate on the glass-topped coffee table, careful not to spill on the eggplant-colored microfiber cushions or her new dress.

She and Adam fed each other tidbits, his breath quickening when she closed her mouth around his thumb and licked a smear of peanut sauce. He shifted in his seat uncomfortably and adjusted his napkin to cover his lap.

Bridget purposely turned her upper body to brush her breasts against his shoulder. "Do you have anything else for me?" She brushed some crumbs off the napkin, noting with satisfaction how his erection rose against her hand.

With a quick motion, he tossed the napkin on the table and pulled her onto his lap. "I do have something else for you."

He sure did. Even through her full skirt, his erection pressed into her bottom. She wiggled slightly until he reached for his plate again.

"Open wide." Adam brushed her lips with a plump strawberry. The topping caught on her upper lip, leaving a dot of chocolate. She licked it off, enjoying how his eyes darkened to the same shade as the chocolate. He teased her with the fruit again, slipping it in and out of her mouth in a sensual rhythm.

She caught his wrist and bit into the berry. He winced theatrically and kissed the side of her mouth, lapping a bit of juice. "Sweet, succulent lips."

Bridget offered him a bite and kissed him full on the mouth. "Your lips, too." He was tart and sweet all at once.

He nuzzled her shoulder. "Let's say our good-byes, Bridget. I've got strawberries at home for a more private dessert."

She was about to agree when Sugar came to the front of the room. "I'd like to thank you all for coming to my housewarming party. Your support and friendship means so much to me and that deserves a treat."

She shut the floor-to-ceiling blinds in front of her picture windows and signaled for the lights to be dimmed. The track lighting lit the space in front of them like a stage. A waiter placed a glossy black chair in the center.

Bridget snuggled under Adam's arm, his body heat warming her bare shoulders. "Is someone putting on a show?"

He shrugged, not really paying attention as he played with a blond ringlet brushing her cheek. "Seems so."

Sugar turned to the guests. "And now, a surprise—my very good friend Anastasia and her handsome partner Lorenzo have agreed to perform their nightclub act for us. They have just returned from their European tour where they stunned audiences in Amsterdam, Hamburg and Frankfurt."

That was an interesting combination of cities. Didn't anyone visit Paris anymore? Adam sighed and she poked him in the ribs. The couple would probably tell some jokes, sing some show tunes and then she and Adam could call it a night.

A lanky woman with spiky platinum-blond hair walked to stand next to Sugar. She was dressed in what looked like a competitive dance costume, a low-cut halter dress with slits high on her thigh. The white sequined material had several cutout areas that allowed her tanned skin to peek through.

Her partner was equally lean but dark-haired and wearing tight black pants and a black silk shirt opened almost to the waist. They clasped hands and bowed as slow, dreamy saxophone music piped from hidden speakers.

They moved into a sinuous step, twining around each other in flashes of black on white. He pulled her into a spin and caught her in his arms. His hand landed firmly on her breast.

Bridget blinked, wondering if his move was a mistake. But the woman didn't look shocked or surprised. Instead, she pressed into his chest and laced her fingers behind his neck. He cupped her breast, pinching her nipple through the fabric. She rotated her hips into his groin.

Just then the woman dropped the top of her dress with a swift movement, baring her breasts.

"What kind of nightclub do they work at?" Adam asked.

"More like a sex club."

He groaned. "Of course—Amsterdam, Hamburg and Frankfurt have the biggest red-light districts in Europe."

"And you know this how?" She raised her eyebrows.

"Purely hearsay." He grinned.

"Looks like those places will *remain* hearsay if I have anything to say about it."

"And you do." He took her hand and kissed it. She ran her fingertips over his jaw, enjoying the slight prickle of his skin.

"Glad to know it." Bridget glanced sideways at Adam.

He caught her eye and turned. "Do you want to leave, Bridget?"

She looked around the room to gauge the others' reactions, not wanting to seem like a hick. Jinx and Electra snuggled with a couple of Sugar's male guests, the room too dark to read their expressions. Sugar sat on her current boyfriend's lap—she'd met him through her accountant. He was tall and handsome with glasses, and he only had eyes for Sugar.

Anastasia spun to face Lorenzo and arched backward ever so slowly, a pale bow against his dark arrowlike straightness. He supported her weight with his hands in the small of her back, leaving her hands free to caress her body.

Bridget had never seen anything like it. The woman's eyes were closed as she drew into her own private fantasy, completely ignoring the dozen strangers watching her avidly.

It was the exact opposite of Bridget's friends' performances at Frisky's. They opened themselves up to interact with the audience and drew them in with the force of their stage personas. Bridget had the feeling that this woman would act the same way in public or private, her confidence like a magnet.

"No, let's stay, at least for a while." She kissed his neck. "I'm finding this inspirational."

"So am I." His erection had grown even harder. "But only because I'm thinking of you instead."

The music changed slightly and Lorenzo gracefully helped Anastasia to straighten. She pulled his shirt loose. He shrugged it off and stood before her bare-chested. He was built slighter than Adam, not having his breadth of shoulder.

Bridget slipped her hand between Adam's buttons, finding a nipple to play with like the woman onstage. His breath hissed and he shifted under her.

"You want to play, sweetheart?" he murmured, sliding his hand into her bodice to cup her breast. "No bra. Nice."

"Sewn in." It was a backless dress after all. The

man had no idea about constructing clothes, preferring only to know how to get her out of them. That was fine with her, considering how he was kneading and thumbing her nipple. She stifled a moan.

The male performer spun his partner away from him and gripped her waist with his hands. She began a long, languorous series of fan kicks, where her legs made wide sweeping circles, her ankle stretching over her head. From where she sat, Bridget didn't think the dancer was wearing anything under that dress.

The sequence ended with Anastasia in splits leaning on her partner, one ankle resting on his shoulder. He pulled up her skirt and fondled the firm tanned globes of her bottom.

Adam squeezed Bridget's bottom through the fabric. She shifted position and pulled his hand to her stocking-covered knee.

He immediately slid his hand up her thigh to the elastic band of her stocking. "Keep going?" he whispered.

She nodded, almost wiggling in anticipation for what he'd find. Or rather, wouldn't find. She knew the exact instant he'd discovered her secret because he froze.

"No panties, either?" He pressed a kiss to her bare shoulder, his dark brown gaze never leaving hers.

She shook her head, so daring, sitting on his lap

with his hands on her breast and between her thighs, although no one could see in the cocoon of darkness.

He insinuated a finger between her curls, his white teeth showing in a grin as he discovered her dampness. Leisurely and languidly in time to the music, his caresses mimicked the sweeping blues beat.

Lorenzo sat on the black chair, his thighs spread wide. Anastasia straddled his lap to face him. By now, her white dress was a mere band around her waist, her breasts and bottom bare. The strip of cloth made it more erotic than if she'd been totally naked.

Bridget writhed against Adam, the woman's gyrations inspiring her. Adam responded with faster touches, his cock growing even harder. She leaned on his chest and he nipped at her earlobe, sucking and teasing her. "Like when my mouth is between your thighs," he whispered.

She started to moan, which he muffled with a hard kiss. Her lips would be puffy, but she didn't care. She broke away, gasping for air. As she turned her head, she saw Anastasia stand and, with a smooth movement, unzip Lorenzo's pants. Naturally, he wasn't wearing a stitch under them, either.

"Holy cow." Her eyes widened. Go ahead and call her a hick, but she'd never expected the show would go this far.

Adam peered around her shoulder. "Well, shit."

The woman sank gracefully to her knees, her mouth widening into an O.

Bridget looked away before she hit her target. Adam shook his head, in half amusement, half exasperation. "I'm not gonna sit here and watch strangers have sex when we could be having some of our own. Let's go." He set her on her feet and dragged her toward the guest bedroom where they'd left their coats.

"But we didn't say our goodbyes to our hostess," she protested once they'd rounded the corner.

He smiled. "Your polite Wisconsin manners won't work here, honey. What would you say, anyway? 'Loved the buffet and the sex show'? Besides, Sugar's wrapped up with that guy of hers. He's feeling pretty happy right now with her hands inside his pants."

They found the guest bedroom, where a pair of bronze sconces illuminated the sage-green walls. Quiet jazz music from the performance filtered into the cozy space. "What about you? Do you want me to do that?"

"Hell, yeah. Once I get you home, you can do whatever you want." He dug through the pile of coats on the queen-size bed to find her wrap.

"I don't want to go home." She touched his arm and he stopped. "I can't wait."

He moved toward the door. "Here? With all those people down the hall?"

She took a big breath and nodded, desire warring with embarrassment. Desire won. "I don't care." She was pretty sure Sugar wouldn't care, either.

"This condo is a loft, you know. Noises travel." His voice was low and husky as he approached her. "You would have to be very quiet. Unless you do want them to know what I'm doing to you here."

She licked her dry lips. "I'll be quiet."

"All right." He pointed to a dark door in the corner. "That's probably the bathroom. Look for a condom and wait for me there."

Bridget took another deep breath and nodded. She tottered to the door and flipped on the switch. She opened a drawer in the vanity topped with an ultra-trendy bowl-style sink. No condoms there.

The medicine cabinet next to the gargantuan mirror yielded several foil packets. She picked one and caught her reflection. Her cheeks and lips had pinkened under Adam's touch, and she was sure some of her blush had come from the etiquette no-no of rifling through her hostess's medicine cabinets.

On the other hand, compared to having semipublic sex in Sugar's bathroom, looking for a condom was small potatoes. Nope. She just couldn't go through with it. A quick cab ride, and they'd be in the privacy of Adam's apartment.

But there he was behind her in the bathroom, wrapping his arms around her waist to nibble her neck.

"Oh, Adam." She giggled at the touch of his lips. One hand slipped into her bodice and the other slowly hiked up her skirt. She tried to relax into him, but the bright light above them and the wide-open door put a crimp in her pleasure. "Close the door."

"No." He found the bare band of thigh above her stocking and rubbed her around and around, palming her buttock. Once, his fingers almost reached where she wanted them to, but he always pulled back. She moaned and rolled her head on his shoulder. But still, that open door…

"Adam, the door."

He increased his caresses. "I said no, Bridget." His voice was low and soft. "Admit it, sweetheart. You've changed since you've been working with those strippers. Wondering what it would be like to dance topless, using me as your willing subject."

She ground into his cock. "And you were more than willing."

"And now tonight." His breath came faster. "Watching those dancers touch each other while I touched you. You want to know what it would be like to make love in front of strangers."

"No," she quickly denied, but he was relentless.

"On a bright stage, mirrors everywhere reflecting your naked, aroused image." Before she could react, he unhooked her halter top from around her neck. It fell to her waist, baring her breasts.

"Adam." She tried to cover herself but he pulled her hands away.

"Look at yourself," he insisted. She knew what she would see—two breasts in serious need of a bra. But he kept her arms pinned to her sides until she looked. Not at herself at first, but at Adam's hungry expression in the mirror. Her nipples tightened before their eyes, pulling and crinkling into firm peaks.

"Don't you dare hide yourself." He released her wrists and slowly cupped both breasts, her flesh overflowing in his palms. He massaged the delicate tissue, drawing a deep groan from her.

She swayed to the rhythm of the faint music coming from the living room. Adam followed her cue, pulling her even closer. His finger flashed across a nipple and the breath whooshed from her.

"You like that?" That tease, he knew darn well she liked it.

"Maybe." She played as coy as she could, considering.

"Should I stop?" He dropped his hands away.

"No!" She grabbed his hands and placed them on her breasts, squeezing. He gave her a cocky grin and rolled her nipples between his fingers. She shuddered, closing her eyes against the bright lights.

"Open your eyes, Bridget," he murmured. "You have to watch. See what your audience sees."

Helplessly, she opened her eyes. Adam's hands

were strong and tanned on her milk-white skin. Her nipples had turned darker pink, almost a dusty rose, as they peeped from between his fingers.

He toyed with her for several minutes. Bridget's breath came harder as she turned her head restlessly on his shoulder. His touch drove her higher and higher, her clit throbbing in time to her racing heart.

"Touch me." She tried to drag his hand under her skirt but he resisted.

"No, you." He nipped her earlobe, stifling her protest. "Your audience wants to see you touch yourself."

She cast a nervous glance toward the open door that led to the bedroom. No one was there.

"Come on, sweetheart. Show us your pretty little puss."

Her eyes widened with shock and her face heated. But Adam gave her a challenging look. She slowly raised her skirt to the tops of her stockings.

"Higher."

She took a deep breath and pulled it to her waist. Like Anastasia, she was bare top and bottom, with only her dress bunched around her middle.

He gave a low whistle. "Beautiful."

She sneaked a peek. The dark blond curls between her thighs were visibly damp, the swollen pink lips peeking through. She knew he was waiting for her to chicken out, but Bridget was no chicken.

"Touch yourself." His face was taut and stern with desire. Tucking her skirt to the side, Bridget ran her hand up her thigh and around the elastic band of her stocking. Her skin was softer than the stocking, especially the soft wedge leading into the crease of her thigh.

"Show me how you want to be touched."

Obeying almost against her will, she slid her hand over to cover her mound. Taking a deep breath, she pressed a finger inside. The merest brush of her fingertip on her clitoris sent a jolt through her. She increased the pace until she was shuddering in his arms.

"Did you like it when that guy did this?" Adam slipped a hand to her bare bottom, squeezing it like they'd seen the performers do.

"Yesss." The word hissed out as he went one further than the performer and slid two fingers in and out of her drenched passage. She clenched around him and he sped up. He added a third finger, and she squealed at the pressure, almost as thick as his cock. She managed to caress her clit as her silk skirt curled against her thighs, a ribbonlike caress. He pinched a nipple with his free hand, the sharp sensation ripping her self-control. She unraveled in his arms and turned her face to muffle her cries in his jacket.

He held her tight, his fingers still moving inside her, determined to wring every drop of her response.

Slowly, she opened her eyes to see Adam's wicked smile. He pulled his fingers free and sucked the tips. "Delicious. But show me more."

He wanted more, he'd get more. Determined to wipe that smug look off his face, she quickly unzipped the side of her dress and shimmied out of it. Wearing nothing but her stockings and heels, she kept her back to him and stepped between him and the sink.

His nonchalant air was finally starting to crack. "Well, my new exhibitionist, what's your next move?"

Ooh, her next move. She rotated her hips into him, his wool trousers rubbing her bottom. He grabbed her hips and stopped her. "Enough teasing. We want to see all of you."

Bridget slowly spread her folds to show him the goods. She was swollen and pink, her clitoris peeping like a pearl button and pulsing gently after her orgasm. She stared at his reflection; he inadvertently licked his lips. Gotcha. Not even the girls at Frisky's went this far.

His fingers dug into her butt. "Damn it, Bridget."

"You like it? My pretty little puss?" She stroked herself slowly and deliberately. The erotic words felt strange on her tongue, but the effect was well worth it.

"I love it." He let go of her and frantically undid his pants, releasing his cock and quickly protecting himself. "Tip your sweet ass up to me."

Bridget braced her hands on the cold, smooth countertop and arched. He cupped her breasts and filled her with a swift stroke. She cried out and he groaned.

He was divine, thick and hot inside her. She hung her head and panted for air, so aroused she wouldn't even care if the UW-Madison Badger marching band came parading through the guest room.

"Look, baby. You've got to see yourself."

She looked in the mirror. Her cheeks were flaming pink, her pupils so dilated that only a rim of burning blue showed. A bead of perspiration trailed down her temple, but hey, her hair was still pulled into an elaborate 'do. She giggled. Superholding power during raunchy semipublic sex wasn't exactly a testimonial the hairspray company could use.

And Adam was doing some superholding of his own, his hands warm and teasing on her breasts as he rocked his cock in and out. Her heels put her at exactly the right height for him to hit the right spot deep inside her. He was so big and dark behind her, appearing fully clothed. His black shirt was still buttoned and his only bare flesh was currently making her insides swoon.

What if she *were* a dancer at Frisky's? She'd dance onstage and catch his hungry stare as she bared her body, thinking only of him. Then he'd request a lap dance in a private room, and she'd cheat a bit and touch his rock-hard penis and let him suck on her nipples, enough to make them both desperate.

She'd dance her next set, horribly turned on and making a ton of tips because the men could sense her genuine arousal. After, she'd run to the dressing room so she could go home and release the howling tension, but before that, Adam would step from the shadowy hall. Without saying a word, they'd find a dark corner and take each other like animals, grunting and moaning as he pulled aside her soaking G-string and shoved his cock deep within her, not caring if anyone was watching as he screwed her hard....

"Oh, Bridget, you're such a bad girl," he whispered, echoing her thoughts. "Somebody might be sitting in the dark, watching me thrust into you. Watching you so hot and turned on that you can't wait to close the door.

"Maybe your beautiful face turns them on so much, they're starting to touch themselves. I should know." His voice changed from husky to wry.

"Why?" She glanced over her shoulder at him.

"Call me a pervert, but I've fantasized about you for years." He thrust harder as he revealed his most private thoughts. "Imagining what color your nipples were, your skin…"

Bridget touched her clit, her nail brushing his erection. "What else?" She'd imagined him for years, too.

"How your ass would grind into me as I pumped hard, the scent and taste of you…"

She grabbed his balls firmly, the way he liked it. He groaned loudly, but she was too caught up to care about the noise carrying. "Did you touch yourself?"

"All the time." She slipped a finger behind his balls and pressed. "Oh, Bridget!" His cock jerked deep inside her.

"When?"

"Ah…" She lessened the pressure to let him answer. "Colin's wedding. Dark purple strapless bridesmaid dress. Your breast popped out during the chicken dance. Took a long, soapy shower that night."

"You should have told me. I would have sneaked off with you to show you more than just a glimpse of breast. Maybe like this, a nearby powder room…" Dancing with him that night, she'd barely resisted the urge to rub herself all over him.

"Bridget, my balls were as purple as your dress."

"Not tonight. Show me what you would have done then."

"This." He fondled both her breasts with one hand, rolling her nipples on his palm. He dropped his other hand to her clit and expertly plucked at it. She swallowed a scream as he coaxed the already sensitized nerves to a pulsing knot.

Her hands slammed on the vanity top as she thrust

desperately back onto him. He tongued her spine, his black shirt clinging to both of them. His cock swelled to stretch her even farther.

Their breathing was harsh and fast in the small bathroom. They couldn't last much longer. She sobbed as he bit her shoulder, like the wild animal she'd made him. His gesture of possession shredded her last bit of self-control. She was now as wild as he was, crying his name in a loud voice as she came. Everything in her being coalesced around his touch, from his shaft deep inside her to his big hands on her breasts to his hot breath on her skin. She was filled and swallowed up by his maleness, wanting to never be free of it.

He shouted her name and followed her, the rhythmic pulses of his orgasm prolonging hers until she collapsed onto the sink.

"Wow, sweetheart." He rested his forehead on her back, panting.

"Wow is right." The cool granite top felt wonderful on her overheated skin. "So, you got to live out your sneaking-off-with-the-bridesmaid fantasy."

"You mean my sneaking-off-with-Bridget fantasy. There's a difference, you know." He kissed the nape of her neck. "A huge difference."

Bridget didn't know what to say. Adam had fantasized about her for years, just as she had about him. Had desire moved into affection for him, as well? Before she got the nerve to ask, he straightened.

"Better get going, hon. The guests will want their coats soon."

So much for fantasy—it was back to practicality. They cleaned up as best they could. Bridget's legs were so wobbly, she almost fell off her high heels, but Adam steadied her and even zipped her into her dress.

"Usually you only help me out of my clothes, not into them," she teased, recalling the thought he'd had earlier.

"Considering how heated up that crowd was, I don't want to take any chances." He found her shawl among the other guests' coats and settled it gently around her shoulders. He rubbed a spot over her shoulder blade.

"What is it?" She craned her head to look.

"I've marked your skin." He looked regretful. "I'll try not to next time."

She grabbed his shirtfront and planted a hard kiss on his mouth. "Don't you dare. I want you wild."

"You make me wild, Bridget." He kissed her until they heard noises at the guest-room door.

"Someone's coming for a coat." She reached for the bedroom door with a shaky hand but it didn't open. "You locked the door?"

"Of course I locked it. I wanted to give you your fantasy, but I didn't want some loser leering at you."

"Oh, Adam." That warmed her better than her wrap. Adam grinned and unlocked the door. The doorknob turned under his fingers.

"Hey, you two." Sugar's puzzled expression quickly turned into a grin. "After you two rushed out during the show, I thought you'd gone home."

Bridget futilely fought her blush but drew up her dignity. "Without saying goodbye to our hostess?"

Behind her, Adam muffled a snicker. She ignored him and kissed her friend's cheek. "Well, Sugar, thank you for the lovely party. The buffet and the sex show were superb."

Giving their fellow guests a sweet smile, she swept out the front door, Sugar's whoops of laughter following them. A poleaxed Adam trailed, stunned, in her wake. Despite what he said, polite Wisconsin manners *did* work everywhere.

9

"THAT IS SO EXCITING!" A deafening squeal zipped through the dancers' undressing room at Frisky's. Bridget winced and covered her ears as Sugar pulled her into a bear hug. It was the first time Bridget had hugged a topless woman, but after all that she'd seen at Frisky's, *qué será, será,* as another busty blonde used to sing.

"I absolutely love Richard's on Rodeo! And you made the finals for his design contest?"

"Yeah, I got the call this afternoon." Bridget grinned, still disbelieving the good news. When she had phoned Adam to tell him, she had almost hyperventilated from excitement. He was taking her out for a celebratory dinner once she completed Sugar's costume fitting.

She urged Sugar in front of the mirror to put the finishing touches on her newest outfit. Sugar was going to be Titania, the fairy queen, complete with wand, wings and see-through glittery gauze dress. Sugar turned obediently as Bridget pinned the seams.

She wouldn't sew the seams, only sew in Velcro later for a rip-away effect.

Sugar sighed in rapture. "Richard's has the most wonderful lingerie. Very sexy but pricey. One of my boyfriends bought me a couple bra-and-panty sets, but that was before my surgery, so the bras don't fit anymore." Sugar winked at her. "Although if you win that contest, maybe you'll get a discount. Men lo-o-o-ve what a Richard's bra does for the ol' ta-tas."

Bridget snickered. "I'll have to keep that in mind."

"Seriously, your bras are as nice as Richard's. I'm not surprised you're in the finals." Sugar bopped her on the shoulder with her wand. "I dub thee Lady Bridget of the Bras, Booster of the Bazoombas."

Bridget poked her in the butt with a straight pin, making her jump and squeal yet again.

"Bridget?" a female voice rasped.

She looked up from the fairy wings she was fitting on Sugar. "Oh, hi, Marge. How are you?"

"Fine, fine." The bottle-redheaded house manager waved her hand dismissively. She took her responsibilities very seriously and always dressed in neat, if inexpensive, professional garb. She still couldn't resist the super high-heeled shoes, though. Bridget wondered if her Achilles tendons had shortened, leaving her feet in a permanent high-heel shape, kind of like a Barbie doll. "What on earth are you girls up to? I gotta warn you, I don't hold with any of that 'Girls Gone Wild' stuff back here."

"What, save it for the customers?" Bridget winked at Sugar, who gave her a wry grin.

"I'll have you know I have delicate sensibilities." Her lofty tones were interrupted by a hacking cough.

Sugar rubbed the older woman's narrow shoulders. "Oh, pooh, Marge, you can't fool us. You could make a sailor blush."

"I've done plenty of things to sailors, but I don't think I ever made them blush." Marge cackled, her amusement so infectious that Bridget and Sugar both joined in.

"Marge used to dance at the clubs around Great Lakes Naval Air Station, when it was open," Sugar explained.

"And I was the belle of the fleet, lemme tell you. But I didn't come in here to intimidate you girls with my long, successful career." She turned to Bridget. "The boss has seen you around and wanted to know if you were interested in being a dancer."

Bridget sat on her heels, stunned. "Me? A dancer?" She caught herself from saying "stripper." Some girls were sensitive about that word.

Marge shrugged. "Yeah, he likes your looks. Says some patrons really go for the natural type."

"Told you," said Sugar, adjusting the glittery strip of near-transparent tulle across her breasts. "Natural

breasts are harder to find in this business than naturally blond hair."

Marge chuckled. "And you ain't got neither, Sugar."

The dancer shrugged. "What I have works for
me." She turned to Bridget, her costume brushing
Bridget's face. "What do you think?"

Stripteasing for Adam or playing exhibitionist
games with him was different. She studied her friend.
"Well, you've told me about sharing a small inner part
with the audience and walling off the rest of yourself."

"Yeah, that's pretty much it. They don't deserve
the important part." Sugar made a moue of disgust,
and Marge nodded.

Bridget shook her head. "No. I don't want to split
myself that way. I want all of me, for me. And Adam."

Sugar gave her a small smile. "Adam." She turned
to Marge. "Her boyfriend would never go for it."

The older woman nodded. "Most men don't. They
don't want other guys looking at what belongs to
them."

Bridget started to protest that she didn't belong to
Adam, but stopped herself. Maybe Sugar understood
her reluctance to mess with her mind that way, but
Marge wouldn't get it. She smiled at Marge. "Tell
him thank you. I'm flattered, but I'll have to decline."

"I figured." She pointed a nicotine-stained finger
at Bridget's work in progress. "Stick to makin' those
pretty costumes. Less grief for you down the road."

Bridget's heart twisted at Marge's wistful expression. Apparently being the belle of the fleet had its downside. She stood and walked over to her suitcase. "You know, Marge, I have a blouse in here for a class project that I cut too small." She pulled out a white top and held it up to the older woman. "Would you like to have it?"

"Me?" She gave Bridget a suspicious look.

"Sure. It's too small for Sugar or me but it looks like it would fit you perfectly."

Marge touched the fine cotton ruffles with the tip of her red nail. "Well, if you're sure…"

"Absolutely. It'll go to the thrift store if you don't want it."

"In that case, I'll take it off your hands." Marge stroked the cotton again, a gleam in her faded brown eyes.

Bridget handed her the blouse and she carried it away to her office.

"Bridget, you softie." Sugar was shaking her head in exasperation. "Wasn't that the blouse Jinx ordered?"

"She wasn't expecting it until next week. I'll make her another."

"Better make it look different than Marge's or Jinx'll have a fit. Good thing you *aren't* going to be a dancer. The others would eat you alive."

Bridget grinned. Being with Adam made her more alive than anything.

"I STILL CAN'T BELIEVE you planned this with a couple hours' notice. I only called you with my good news at four o'clock." Adam had surprised Bridget with a fancy French dinner, and now a cozy horse-and-carriage ride down Michigan Avenue. It was the one time she didn't mind looking at the tail end of a farm animal.

"You know me, Bridget. I'm a quick-thinking guy." He grinned at her. "I had this organized ten minutes after you hung up." He brushed a stray curl off her bare neck. Tonight she'd chosen to wear an off-the-shoulder black satin top with corset lacing up the back with a matching wrap. Her own design, of course.

He poured them each a flute of champagne and raised his glass. "To the hottest designer in Chicago—and the hottest woman, too."

Bridget laughed. "Thank you, Adam." The clink of their champagne glasses sounded over the clip-clop of the horse's hooves. It was the most romantic gesture anyone had ever made for her and her happiness bubbled up like the sparkling wine.

She sighed and gazed up at the dark skyscrapers. They were even more awe-inspiring up close. She absolutely loved living in the city. "I can tell why they call this the Magnificent Mile. I've never seen it so beautiful."

He nuzzled her ear. "Not as beautiful as you, Bridget."

She turned to him and smiled. Streetlight glinted

off his black hair and his deep brown eyes gazed into hers. "Oh, Adam. I never guessed you had such a romantic streak."

"I usually don't," he confessed, twirling the flute between his strong fingers. "But you deserve all the best things in life, sweetheart. Sometimes I think you're too good for me." He winked at her but she narrowed her eyes.

"'Too good for me'? What does that mean?" She had a sneaking suspicion it was because of his up-bringing. "Because of your past?"

"My past?" He sat up, startled.

"Your parents," she clarified.

"Oh, them." He relaxed back into the cushions. "Yeah, we weren't exactly the Waltons, like you guys."

Bridget snickered. "Despite being deprived of 4:00 a.m. wake-ups, being whacked in the face by dirty cow tails and shoveling enough manure to fer-tilize the entire state of Wisconsin, I think you turned out just fine."

"That still remains to be seen." Leaning forward, he flipped open a small cooler. "Strawberries are included, but if we don't eat them on our ride, we can save them for later." He winked at her again and drank his champagne.

Bridget let him change the subject and sipped her own drink. The breeze off Lake Michigan made her shiver, and Adam was quick to wrap his arm around her shoulders. "Better?"

She leaned on him. "With you, always."

ADAM UNLOCKED his front door. "I'm back!" He loved coming home to Bridget, even if he'd only been in the lobby for three minutes getting his morning newspaper and mail.

She waved to him from the dining room, a watering can in hand as she doused her plants. He'd never had any plants that weren't on the Drug Enforcement Agency's controlled substances list, but Bridget's actually cheered up his mostly black-and-beige décor. Just like Bridget herself did.

She set down the watering can. "Oh, I want to see if the stores are having sales on spring fashions yet."

In handing her the newspaper, he accidentally dropped his mail. She bent for it, her jeans snug across her ass. Then he noticed the official-looking envelope.

Unfortunately, she spotted it, too. "Internal Revenue Service." She held out the envelope. "Oh, look, Adam. Your tax refund check came in the mail today."

He sped around the corner to the kitchen. "Thanks." He stuffed the envelope in his pocket. "Want some coffee?"

"It's decaf for your blood pressure, so don't get your hopes up. Aren't you going to open it? I got my tax refund direct-deposited a few weeks ago." She frowned. "I thought you filed online. Don't you get yours direct-deposited?"

"Uh…" He hated to see the puzzled look on her face and sighed. May as well confess the whole stupid mess with his parents. At least it wouldn't be too much of a shock, considering Bridget had unfortunately met them a couple times.

"Come with me." He led her to the couch and sat. Opening the envelope, he scanned the letter. Pretty much what he'd expected, the IRS confirming payment for part of his parents' tax evasion fine. He passed it to her.

She read it silently, her expression growing more and more pissed off. She finally looked at him. "And you went along with this?"

"Hey, why are you mad at me?" He thought she'd be mad at his parents. He was the good guy, the one who was bailing them out.

"Oh, I'm mad at them, too. But you should know better—you live and breathe finance. Why on earth did you agree to pay the IRS this kind of money?" She shook the letter at him. "Ten thousand dollars? Did you wipe out your whole savings for them?"

"Yeah, it was pretty much what I could get my hands on." He'd stood firm on not cashing in his investments, though.

She jumped to her feet and tossed the letter at him. "This is terrible, Adam."

His eyes widened. She hardly ever got this angry.

"What did they ever do for you that they deserve ten thousand dollars of your hard-earned money?"

He raised his palms. "Um…they didn't leave me to starve. Or sell me for black-market adoption." Or to one of their pervert friends.

"I'm not joking, Adam." She put her hands on her hips.

"Neither am I, Bridget."

She stopped mid-rant and looked at him thoughtfully. "It was really that bad?"

He nodded. "I know you think I was exaggerating about the whole marijuana thing when we were at the conservatory, but it *was* that bad. The biker parties when I was a preschooler, the closet pot greenhouse when I was in middle school, the time they took off for Sturgis and left me with fifteen dollars and six cans of pork and beans."

"Six cans of pork and beans?"

"At least no one was around to complain about the gas."

She shook her head at his feeble joke. "Oh, Adam. What a rotten thing to do to a kid."

"No argument here." At least he'd avoided the foster-care system.

"So why bail them out?" She crumpled the IRS envelope in her fist.

"As a goodbye." His path had finally become

clear. He'd heard some radio shrink blather on about toxic people, and ten thousand dollars was a price he was willing to pay for detox.

"Goodbye?"

Despite all her grumbling about her parents and brothers he was sure she would rather lose a body part than lose her family. But his parents were more like a precancerous mole that needed to be removed. Or maybe a tapeworm.

Adam put his arm around her. "I figure this makes me and them even. For all the years they spent bitching about me costing so much to raise, they can have it back. They don't owe me and I don't owe them."

She looked sad and slowly nodded. "You're right. You don't owe them a thing. But if they came to you changed people, just wanting a relationship, not money, would you accept them?"

He gave her a wry smile. His Bridget, still sweet and innocent despite her more sophisticated outer trappings. His parents had seen him only as a liability when he was younger and dependent on them, and then as a bank once he was financially independent. But if she actually thought they might have a change of heart, who was he to disillusion her? "Yes. If they wanted to develop an actual parental-type relationship with me, I would be open to that." And he might also hit the lottery someday without buying a ticket.

"Good, I suppose. Because however dreadful they might be, they're still your parents."

He laughed. "Dreadful—now that's a good word to describe them."

"My mother's." Bridget ran her hand along his arm.

"My goodness, such language," he teased. Mrs. Weiss had once grabbed Col by the ear for uttering "damn" in her presence.

"She feels rather strongly about your parents."

"And how does she feel about me?" He was glad to get off the subject of his parents.

"She's always asking Colin and Dane when you're coming home for a visit. Mom *loves* you." Bridget seemed a bit embarrassed and looked away. She patted his knee briskly. "Well, anyway, let's get going to that bakery." She strode off to grab her windbreaker. "Come on, if I don't eat something frosted in the next ten minutes, I won't be responsible for my actions."

He stood, bemused by her rapid departure, coming right on the heels after she'd told him her mom loved him. Was that it? Did the L-word make her awkward? It wasn't his favorite word, either.

They were two friends who were using each other to stave off loneliness in the big city. They might be lovers, but not in love. And that little added *r* and *s* made all the difference in the world.

10

BRIDGET SAT UP STRAIGHT from where she'd been hunching over a particularly tricky jacket pattern and stretched her neck and shoulders. She pushed away from the Ping-Pong table and wandered over to her fridge to grab a ginger ale. The green cans were the only thing in her apartment fridge aside from various condiments.

She and Adam ate almost all their meals together. It had been the best time of her life. Recalling their past few weeks together made her press the cold can against her hot cheeks. Whew, she needed to finish her sewing and get home to Adam.

Home to Adam. She giggled. What would a real home with Adam be like? Maybe a cozy city house with a backyard for her to plant some flowers. Maybe a hammock between two old trees for them to snuggle in and gaze at whatever passed for stars in the city. Just what she wanted.

But not what Adam wanted. The image of a Wisconsin farmhouse popped to mind, the scent of manure wafting into the kitchen as she fought with creaky appliances trying to feed a hungry dairy farmer and farmhands. Been there, done that. Her mother hadn't even gotten a dishwasher until Bridget was in high school. A dishwasher besides Bridget, that is. Her brothers had been suspiciously butterfingered in the kitchen until her exasperated mother banned them from KP.

The whole city mouse/country mouse thing was getting too depressing to contemplate any further, so she swigged back her pop and dug in her bag to see if Adam had called. Ooh, a voice mail had come in while her sewing machine had been humming along. She dialed and pressed her password to listen.

"Bridget, this is your father. Call me."

Hmm. She hoped it wasn't bad news. Her father wasn't the type of guy to call to chitchat. Since he had called her from his cell phone, she called him on that number.

"Weiss."

She heard cows mooing in the background and an unexpected wave of homesickness hit her. "Hi, Dad, it's Bridget."

"Oh, hey there. How're ya doing?"

."Fine, Dad. Keeping busy. I got your message."

"Right, your mother's fiftieth birthday is on the nineteenth."

"Wow, already." She'd totally lost track of things like that.

"Now, you know your mother. She told me not to make a fuss because you and the boys are all plenty busy, but between you and me, a quiet dinner with me at the Korner Café is not what she really wants."

She grinned. Eating at the Korner Café was like eating at home. Her parents never even bothered to look at a menu after thirty-odd years of patronage. "I'll come for her birthday, Dad. Have you made any plans for a party?"

"What with Jenna having her baby in a couple months and the other two little ones, we thought it would be easier to have a lunchtime party, so I made reservations at the country club. Marv said they have a fancy buffet. All you can eat."

And her dad's friend Marv would know. Buffet managers wept when the six-foot-eight dairy farmer walked in the door. She wrote the details as her father gave them. When they'd finished hashing out the party plans, she turned to the problem of actually getting to Wisconsin. "Okay, so I'll rent a car and drive up Friday to spend the weekend. I have a long weekend because of Dead Week, so I don't need to be back until Tuesday."

"Dead Week? What the heck's that?"

"An extra few days to prepare for final projects and exams. No classes or meetings are scheduled during that time." She'd fortunately planned ahead and finished most of her schoolwork already.

"Dead Week, huh? Kinda peculiar, but if it means you can come home for the party, sounds fine to me." He cleared his throat. "She didn't say so specifically, but I know your mother would be tickled pink if Adam Hale can come, too."

"Adam Hale?" She forced a casual note into her voice. "Why? Has Colin or Dane talked to him lately?" She really, really hoped not.

"Dunno about that. But being as how you're in the same city as him, maybe the two of you can drive together."

"I don't know, Dad. From what I hear, Adam has a pretty busy schedule." How were she and Adam supposed to pretend to be just friends around her family for a whole entire long weekend?

"You have his phone number, Bridget. Call him and ask. Your mother's always been fond of him. And it makes me feel better that you're not driving alone in some heap of a rental car."

Bridget sighed quietly. Her dad had unwittingly backed her into a tight spot. "Okay, Dad. I'll try to get a hold of Adam and invite him."

"Sounds good. So we'll see you and Adam later on Friday."

They said their goodbyes and Bridget drummed her fingers on the Ping-Pong table. If her mom wanted Adam invited to her fiftieth birthday party, Bridget would invite him, with the clear understanding that their relationship, whatever it was, was strictly between the two of them.

Her brothers and dad would be clueless as usual, but her mom was one sharp cookie. She'd have to warn Adam to keep his distance and hang out mostly with the guys. She'd keep to the kitchen with her mom and sister-in-law, Jenna. Maybe she could take her niece and nephew for Happy Meals to give Jenna a break.

And Bridget knew for a fact that the farm's plumbing system had plenty of icy-cold water. She and Adam would be using a lot of it.

"WE'RE ALMOST THERE, Bridget." Adam sucked in a big breath of country air. "I swear, this place gets more beautiful every time I visit."

She looked up from her textbook and glanced out the car window. Yep, Wisconsin was pretty, if a bit monotonous. Green hills and black-and-white cows. "Turn right off the highway at the next corner."

"I remember." He smiled at her from the driver's seat. "Visiting here was the highlight of my summer vacation."

"Your chance to get some home cooking, huh?" She made one more note in the margin.

"My chance to see you."

She looked up in surprise but wasn't able to question him before he pulled into the farm's gravel driveway.

He grinned and waved at her parents and Dane, who were approaching the rental car with welcoming shouts. He hastily rolled up the window and looked at her wryly. "Showtime, sweet—I mean, Bridge." He'd reverted to his pre-dating nickname for her and she sighed.

At least being called "Bridge" would remind her of their supposedly platonic relationship. She opened the car door and hopped out into the real, Weiss-based world.

BRIDGET HAD FORGOTTEN how much work Weiss World was, although it was fun to be with her mother, who had maybe slightly more ash than blonde in her hair, but was still plump and cheerful. Her mother had fussed over her like the return of the prodigal son and Adam's reception wasn't too far behind, complete with feasting and large amounts of fatted calf, pork and chicken.

At least the cookout last night had been the guys' responsibility. Her dad, Dane and Adam had all grunted appropriately over Wisconsin's finest brats, red and white, burgers and hot dogs. Her mom had brought buckets of potato salad, coleslaw and cherry and apple crisps. Unfortunately it was too early in the season for local corn on the cob, and her dad refused to eat flavorless grocery-store imports.

Colin and his family hadn't made it for dinner from their farm about forty-five minutes away. Colin's wife, Jenna, hadn't been feeling well and wanted to stick close to home, but they would come to the farm for a short visit before her mother's birthday brunch at one.

Despite any brunch plans, busy farmers still needed breakfast, so Bridget and her birthday-girl mom were awake at the grand hour of six-thirty for meal prep. Bridget yawned as she stood by the stove. She must have gotten used to sharing a bed with Adam because she'd tossed and turned in her childhood twin-size bed all night.

"Bridget, why don't you see if the boys are ready to eat?" Mom pulled a platter of pancakes from the oven where they'd been keeping warm.

"Okay, let me finish the bacon and sausage." She lifted a couple pounds of pork out of the griddle and grabbed a paper towel to blot the grease.

Mom shook her head. "No, no, your dad likes them like that."

She rolled her eyes but dropped the paper towel. She hoped Dad liked his coronary arteries nearly as well. Stepping outside the back door, she rang the iron triangle to summon them inside for breakfast. Her dad was wearing his NEXTEL walkie-talkie, but the heft of the cast-iron beater vibrating into her arm made her feel like she was really at home.

Adam was the first out of the milking barn, adorable in his green plaid flannel shirt and faded-at-the-crotch blue jeans. An old feed-store baseball cap sat incongruously on his trendy city haircut. He grinned as he saw her standing on the porch.

Suddenly everything seemed wonderful just because of his smile. The pink peonies smelled sweeter, the sun shone brighter, and even a hint of birdsong pierced her ear.

He took the porch steps two at a time. "Good morning, sleepyhead." Even though he was at least two feet away from her, awareness sizzled between them like the bacon strips on the griddle.

"Good morning, Adam." Self-conscious about her bedhead and navy-blue sweatpants with a hole in the knee, she smoothed her hair and gave him a small smile in return.

"Hey, Bridge, you finally hauled your ass outta bed!" Dane had followed Adam. It just went to show how wrapped up in Adam she'd been that she hadn't noticed her blond hulk of a brother approaching.

"Good morning to you, too, Danish," she replied, using his old nickname and sticking out her tongue. Adam shook his head and laughed. A blush crept into her cheeks. Twelve hours at home and she was regressing to childish taunts.

"Wash up, boys. Cows are fed, and now it's our turn." Her father came behind Dane, his usual John

Deere cap planted firmly on his head. Bridget knew that once he took it off to eat, he'd sport the typical farmer facial tan with sun-darkened cheeks and pale forehead. She'd noted his hair had receded a little farther since her last visit.

All three toed off their boots before coming inside and went to wash up in the mudroom off the kitchen while Bridget and her mom brought the food into the dining room.

Bridget sat next to her mom, Dane sat next to the food and Adam sat next to her father. Throughout breakfast and cleanup afterward, Adam stuck with the guys, discussing farming with a fair amount of background knowledge. He had obviously been studying since their zoo visit, since he was able to debate the finances of organic versus traditional dairy farming. His agricultural economics degree would serve him in good stead once he started farming. Farming was a numbers game as much as anything else.

Her mother noticed her distraction as they dried and put away the breakfast dishes. "Earth to Bridget."

"What?" She looked over in surprise.

Her mother plucked at the white-and-blue iron-ware milk pitcher from her hands. "You've been drying that pitcher for the past five minutes. It's lasted since your great-grandmother's wedding, but I don't know if the glaze can stand much more rubbing."

"Sorry, Mom." She passed the antique over to her mother with a sheepish smile. "I've got a lot on my mind."

"Such as?"

Bridget blanked for a second. Since coming home to Wisconsin, her thoughts had been full of Adam and his interest in farming, but she couldn't very well say that.

Mom lifted an eyebrow. "So how often do you see Adam in Chicago?"

Yikes, she was perceptive. Time to obfuscate. "We both have very busy schedules, Mom, between his trading job and my classes. Hey, did I tell you I'm a finalist in a lingerie-design contest?"

"That's wonderful, Bridget. But it's not for that trampy pink store in the mall with the huge pictures of half-naked girls in the window, is it?" She crinkled her nose.

Bridget grinned. Her mother did not approve of sex-driven advertising. The one time her brothers had been dumb enough to get that store catalog sent to their house, Mom had whacked each of them in the head with it and burned it on the trash heap. "No, it's for a smaller company based on the West Coast. They have a much classier approach." Unlike Bridget's decidedly *un*-classy stripper outfits. She hoped her mother never learned she was designing tearaway see-through dresses and drop-down breast-cup bodysuits.

"Good. I don't really see what all the fuss is, anyway. All a lady needs is a few nice white cotton bras and maybe a black one for funeral clothes."

Bridget winced. "But, Mom, women need different fabrics and colors for different clothing. Low-cut tops as opposed to T-shirts or sweaters, special-occasion outfits. And it's nearly impossible to find nice bras in larger sizes that are comfortable."

Her mother looked up from where she was wiping the countertop. "We found you plenty of nice bras in larger sizes when you were growing up, remember?"

"Oh, yuck, Mom! Those were maternity bras! One even had hooks to drop the cup for breast-feeding." *That* had been fun, wearing a nursing bra into her middle-school locker room. "That's how I started in lingerie design, by pulling out the hooks and sewing on bows to cover the seams."

Mom looked hurt. "Bridget, we did the best we could. All those satin bras were inappropriate for a girl your age."

"Even the white or light-pink ones?"

"Young girls should stick to plain cotton." Her mother rinsed the dishcloth and hung it over the sink faucet. "But now that you're such a good seamstress, you can make pretty much whatever you want." She came over to Bridget and squeezed her shoulders. "And besides, your old mom doesn't really need to know what you're wearing, does she?"

Bridget laughed. She was actually wearing a black satin-and-lace plunge-cup bra, but if Mom wanted to imagine her in white cotton maternity bras, she wouldn't disabuse her of the notion. If she ever needed a maternity bra at some long-distant date, she'd make sure it was chic and elegant. A nice lined lace?

"So, about Adam…"

Darn it, their detour into Bra Land hadn't diverted her bloodhound of a mother. "What about Adam?" A car honking from the yard caught their attention and Bridget peered out the window. "Hey, it's Colin, Jenna and the kids." Hurrying from the kitchen, eager to see her brother and his family, she practically flew down the porch steps.

"Aunt Bridget!" her niece, Emily, hollered. "Hurry—unbuckle me, Daddy!"

As soon as Col freed her, the blond five-year-old dynamo launched herself from the minivan's sliding door into Bridget's arms. "Ooof, gotcha!"

"Me, too!" Three-year old Michael was a bit more cautious than his sister and made sure Bridget was ready for him.

She swung him out and lugged them onto her hips. "How are my sweeties?" She kissed their soft cheeks, the baby-shampoo scent rising from their heads to tickle her nose. She really needed to get back to Wisconsin more often.

Adam looked over at her from where he was greeting Colin. The kids' excited chatter receded into the background as their gazes locked. Bridget's heart pounded at his intense stare, full of tenderness and affection. *Oh, Adam, stop looking at me that way. You're going to make me fall in love with you.*

"Bridget, can you watch the kids? I've got to get to the bathroom." Her poor sister-in-law didn't wait for an answer as she sprinted into the farmhouse as fast as a seven-months pregnant woman could sprint.

"We had to stop three times for Mommy to pee," Michael informed her in that blunt preschool way of his.

"Mommy said it's more polite to say 'use the bathroom,'" Emily informed him in a big-sister tone. Michael shrugged. A boy who had only recently stopped peeing on Cheerios in the toilet to improve his aim couldn't be bothered with the niceties.

"Hey, Bridge." Her brother Colin wrapped all three in a bear hug. The kids protested and squirmed until he let go. Colin smiled at her, his light-brown hair clipped shorter than when she'd last seen him. He was starting to get crow's-feet around his bright blue eyes from sun and wind exposure.

"Hi, Col." She turned in the direction where Jenna had scurried. "How's she feeling?"

"Tired, has to piss like a racehorse all the time. About what you'd expect."

"Maybe I can keep the kids out of her hair this weekend."

"That'd be nice. Calving season never seemed to end this spring, and Jenna pitched in when we needed."

Bridget shook her head. The heaviest job her sister-in-law should have been doing was to wash a load of baby clothes, but that wasn't the way farm life worked.

And if she was going to keep her sanity and her heart intact, she'd remember *that*, instead of imagining baby-shampooed black hair and tiny sparkling dark eyes that bore a striking resemblance to Adam's.

ADAM CHECKED his watch. You could set a clock by the Weiss family, and today was no exception. Brunch or no brunch, it was time for the daily morning coffee and sweet-roll break, and Mrs. Weiss had laid down a spread worthy of Starbucks. Bridget staggered inside after chasing the kids around the farmyard for more than an hour and went straight to the coffeepot where he was standing. "Ah, sweet caffeinated ambrosia."

"Here you go." He automatically passed her the sugar bowl and cream pitcher. "There should be enough cream in here for you." Bridget liked her coffee so light and sweet it was almost a dessert.

"Thanks, Adam. You have a good memory for how I take my coffee."

Oops. "Oh, uh, I don't. I wasn't sure. So I gave you both." He spun away from her and wandered over to the plate of coffee-cake slices, homemade donuts and apple strudel. What the hell…he was sure getting a better workout here than at his gym in Chicago, so he took one of each.

Bridget's dad, Bob, came up behind him and slapped him on the shoulder. "Help yourself, Adam. You're practically family, anyway."

"Gee, thanks, Mr. Weiss." He tried hard to keep the chagrin from his voice, feeling lower than the cow shit they'd scraped off their boots earlier. This kind of awkwardness on his part was why he'd resisted coming along for the weekend until Bridget had told him her mother specifically invited him.

Fortunately, the older man didn't notice his discomfort and continued, "We all feel better about Bridget moving to Chicago with you there to keep an eye on her. A young gal on her own in the city can get herself into all sorts of trouble."

Holy shit. There were so many pitfalls in that minefield of a sentence he didn't know where to step. Bridget glared over the rim of her coffee cup, her face flush with anger. He didn't want to disagree with her dad, a man he genuinely liked, but Bridget deserved better.

Adam jumped in. "Actually, Bob, Bridget has done fine all by herself. She's paying for all her own tuition and living expenses, getting great grades and even has an interesting part-time job." He figured vagueness about the exact nature of her job was the best plan.

Bridget looked at him in surprise, obviously expecting him to have gone along with her dad. Bob looked surprised, as well. Usually, no one disagreed with him.

Bridget came to stand next to Adam. "My professor sponsored me for a design contest that was only open to third- and fourth-year students, and I'm a finalist. And my special-order clients are very happy with the bras and panties I make for them. Some are very difficult to fit due to their large bust size and—"

"Good, good," her dad interrupted, his already ruddy complexion darkening even further in embarrassment. He cleared his throat. "Anyhow, glad to hear our little girl's succeeding so well. Gonna go check on how your mom's doing in the kitchen." He beat a hasty retreat.

Bridget grinned. "Ha, I knew that would get him. Mention women's underwear and he blushes uncontrollably. And this from a man who looks at udders all day. You'd think mammary glands wouldn't be such a big deal."

"You know they are—that's how you're making your fame and fortune." If he didn't get away from her, he'd kiss her right there in her parents' living room. He purposely sat at the far end of the couch.

"As long as there are out-of-proportion breast implants, I'll never starve," she agreed solemnly before breaking into giggles. "Big bras by Brigitte," she intoned in a haughty French accent.

"Brigitte?"

Bridget had adopted the corny accent to be funny, but now that she considered it, it was a great marketing schtick. "Why not? I don't think Ree-shard is any more French than I am. He's probably plain Richard from Podunksville, U.S.A."

"Hey, you're from Podunksville, too, Bridge." Colin had ambled into the living room carrying a can of Pepsi and flopped onto the couch next to Adam. "No need to be ashamed of being a hick." He swigged some pop and belched.

"Colin!" His wife stood in the doorway, a frown on her pretty face. "Just because you're a hick doesn't mean you need to be disgusting, as well."

He bolted upright. "Sorry, hon." He gave her a placating smile.

"And use a coaster, too." She turned back to the kitchen, grumbling under her breath about slobs setting bad examples for the children.

Bridget snickered and was about to go join Adam on the sofa when he jumped to his feet and gave her a meaningful look. Oh, that's right. They were *not* a couple, at least in front of the family.

Adam circled around her to sit in her dad's armchair and Bridget had to sit next to her brother on the scratchy plaid couch. Fun city. Lacking any Adam-time for the foreseeable future, she decided to needle her brother for old times' sake. "So what's with Jenna? Did you leave your boots on and track manure into the house again?"

"No, not this time. Before we left this morning, I put my coffee cup on the counter and left a ring."

"Horrors!"

"Ha-ha, Bridge. She's been on a cleaning kick for the past week since calving season wound down." He leaned over to her conspiratorially while keeping a wary eye on the kitchen doorway. "I even caught her ironing my briefs. With spray starch."

Laughter bubbled up in her and spilled out. Adam joined in, his laughter booming through the living room.

"Shh!" Colin warned. "I'm not joking. She was so pissed when I complained that I didn't dare rewash them. They were too stiff to wear so I'm, uh, going without," he finished lamely, a bright red hue creeping up his ears.

Bridget edged away from her brother and made a face. Too much information. But Adam howled, sliding off the chair to sit on the blue-and-red braided rag rug. When he could speak again, he raised a teasing face to Colin. "Make sure your fly's zipped up good, Col. You don't want to have one of those farming accidents that makes the supermarket tabloids."

Colin chucked a needlepoint pillow at Adam's head. "Oh, shut up, Adam. At least I use mine for something besides pissing."

There was an awkward silence. "Colin. Your sister's right here." Adam nodded over at her burning face.

"Oh, geez. Sorry, Bridge."

"That's all right." Luckily her brother assumed her blush was from embarrassment, not the fact that she was intimately acquainted with the contents of Adam's fly. Contents that were in jeopardy if her brothers ever learned what exactly she and Adam had been up to in Chicago.

"Try a bit of potato and Daddy will take you to the dessert table, Michael." Bridget scooped some mashed potatoes and gravy and held the spoonful in front of her nephew's mouth. He nibbled at it like a baby bird before eating the whole bite. She sat between him and his older sister, cutting meat and cajoling them into eating some plant matter while her parents and Colin sat at the other end of the table with Adam. Better to put a safe distance between them.

Colin returned from his umpteenth trip to the

steam tables and stopped next to her. "Huh, I thought Jenna'd be done by now." Dane looked up from shoveling food into his mouth and shrugged.

Col leaned down, his plate tipping precariously over her. "Hey, Bridge, can you go see what's keeping Jenna? She hasn't come back from the can yet and she hasn't been feeling so hot the past couple days."

Aside from rolling her eyes at her brother's lack of delicacy, she went to the ladies' room without protest and pushed open the door. "Jenna? Are you okay?"

A whimper answered her and Bridget's heart sank as she flew to the farthest stall. "Jenna!" She banged on the metal door. "Can you unlock the door?"

The latch slowly turned, and Bridget found her sister-in-law crouched on the toilet, her face pale as Swiss cheese. "Oh, thank God it's you." Sweat plastered her light-brown hair to her head. "The pain's started, Bridget. I think I'm going into labor."

11

"NO, DON'T WORRY, we'll take care of everything here on the farm. I do remember how, you know." Bridget gripped her parents' rotary-dial phone and listened to her mother's tense instructions for a minute longer. "Mom, everything will be fine. You concentrate on your end of things, and we'll manage."

After a few more soothing comments, Bridget finally hung up and turned to Adam, who'd shoved his fists into his pockets.

"Is Jenna okay?" His voice fell to a whisper. "How about the baby?"

Bridget all but leapt into his arms. He hugged her so hard her ribs almost cracked. "They're both okay for now. The doctors think she has a bad bladder infection that started her labor, but with some IV fluids and antibiotics, they should be able to stop the baby from coming so soon." Her sister-in-law still had about nine weeks left until her due date. "Jenna's parents are on their way from Branson and should get in the day after tomorrow."

He kissed the top of her head. "Geez, Bridget, I had no idea she was so sick. I feel awful that she was fixing coffee and sweet rolls for us."

"My mom says that Colin's frantic. When they told him they needed to transfer her to the high-risk neonatal unit in Madison, he almost went nuts. Dane's going to stay with him at the hospital while Mom takes care of the kids at Colin's house and Dad milks their cows until Jenna's parents arrive."

"Who's going to milk your dad's cows?"

She grinned at him, her first smile since she'd found poor Jenna huddled in the bathroom. "We are."

"WHAT NOW?" Adam grimaced nervously at the black-and-white flank of the giant Holstein eating her feed next to him.

Bridget handed him a clean cloth. "Wash her teats—like this." She demonstrated on a nearby cow.

He did his best to imitate her, but his cow still shifted uneasily. "Sorry for the cold hands."

Bridget snickered. "Such a gentleman."

"Hey, a lady deserves nice, warm hands on her delicate regions." He grinned over at her.

"Put the teat cups on like this and make sure the pulsator hoses are connected to the claw so everything's nice and snug. My dad said he changed the inflations—the cup liners—last month, so at least we don't have to do that."

"Oh. Good." He did his best to slip the teats into the cups like she showed him, making sure the hoses were hooked up properly. Using a claw for milking sounded painful, but it was just the collection site for milk that supported and connected the teat cups.

Bridget stopped to adjust his work on her way to the next cow in its stall. But this wasn't called a barn. They called it a milking parlor, which was funny because it invoked the images of cows standing around in a lacy Victorian-era room with buckets under their udders. Here the cows were on a raised concrete platform so the people milking them could stand on the lower floor and wouldn't need to bend under the udder.

"Come on, slowpoke. We have another hundred cows to do after this bunch."

Holy crap. And they did this twice a day? Colin even milked his cows three times a day, claiming a higher yield. Even with three milkings a day, Adam bet Bridget's dad would finish before all of them.

"Adam!" Bridget gave him a pointed stare. She had hooked up four cows while he'd stood there spacing out. "This is what you have to do if you want to be a dairy farmer."

He took a deep breath and followed her, wondering if he was in fact cut out to be one.

BY THE END of the next day, Adam wasn't wondering anymore. He knew, for sure, that he was too much of a wimp to hack it in the big, bad world of commercial milk-producing. The only thing he was capable of doing now was sitting in Mr. Weiss's ancient armchair and trying not to whimper while the aspirin kicked in.

"Can I get you a heating pad while you eat your supper?" Bridget came from the kitchen carrying a plate of ham-on-white sandwiches. "You did a lot more than even Dad does. Dad had thought Dane would be around to help so he gave his milking guy a few days off to take his wife on a short vacation."

"You did most of the work, Bridget. I thought I was in shape, but all that bending and hefting feed around was more than I expected." He'd been too tired yesterday evening to do anything but sleep, much to his chagrin.

She sat on the couch and put the plate on the end table between them. "It's a hard life, Adam," she said matter-of-factly. "Mom and Dad have it in their blood. Colin and Jenna, too, especially since Colin took over her parents' farm so they could retire and travel." She picked up half a sandwich and looked at it before setting it down. "I almost wish I wanted to stay on the farm. It would make things easier for me."

"Why? You love fashion and lingerie design. We both know you can't do that here."

She finally looked at him, her blue eyes filling

with tears. "But *you* want to be here. And I want to be with you."

His heart melted. He'd never seen her cry before. "Don't cry, baby. I want to be with you, too. Come here." He reached over to her and took her hand, pulling her onto his lap.

She snuggled into his chest, obviously not minding his cow-and-hay-scented flannel shirt. "I don't know what to do anymore. We have such different ideas, and neither of us should have to compromise."

"So let's not." Adam shrugged, even that small motion causing shoulder pain. "At this point, I don't care if I ever see a cow again, so once Jenna's better and your parents come home, you and I will cruise off to the big city and pick up where we left off."

"Where did we leave off? With me sewing clothes for exotic dancers and you trying not to have the top of your head blow off from your blood pressure?"

"Geez, I don't know, Bridget." He tipped up her chin and kissed her on the nose. "Yeah, career-wise, we could both make some changes, but I meant you and me. We're fine, aren't we?"

"Yeahhh…" She didn't seem convinced, so he nuzzled her neck.

"We *are* fine together." He infused loads of not-so-hidden meaning into his voice and smoothed his hand over her hip. "And I've been dying the past couple of days with you wearing these snug jeans and bending over all sorts of farmy-type things."

That got a smile. "Farmy-type things?"

He cupped her ass and squeezed. "Don't make me get all technical on you, now."

"Is that what they're calling it nowadays?" She squirmed on his lap, her breath coming faster.

"Well, well. Let's go upstairs and find out. We're alone, after all."

"No." She shook her head. "Too weird here in my parents' house." She hopped up and pulled his sorry ass into a standing position. "Come with me. I know the perfect place." She went to the linen closet and took an old blanket.

He ran after her but screeched to a halt in disappointment. "Bridget, I didn't bring any protection with me since I thought your parents would be here all weekend."

She looked over her shoulder and winked. "We should be able to think of something."

BRIDGET HAD BEEN thinking of several somethings since Adam had first visited the farm years ago. Of course, her fantasies then had been rather fuzzy on the details and resembled the love scene from *Gone With the Wind* where the bedroom door had firmly closed before any of the good parts happened. And she fully intended to have all of Adam's good parts tonight.

He stopped at the bottom of the porch stairs and stared at the sky in wonder. "Look at all the stars. I haven't seen this many since the last time I was here."

Bridget followed his lead. "Wow." The sky was a gorgeous midnight black studded with thousands of silvery stars. "Look, there's the Big Dipper and Orion's Belt." She pointed out her favorite constellations to Adam.

"You can see the whole Milky Way from here, can't you?"

"If you can't see the Milky Way in Wisconsin, where *can* you see it?" Certainly not in the city. The night sky in Chicago was usually either gray or a weird orange from all the reflected lights.

"So is this where you had in mind?" He looked around. "Just the two of us under the full moon and stars? Kind of out in the open, but I don't care if you don't."

She laughed and led him across the farmyard, past the modern milking parlor and into the old barn that had stood for the past century. Her parents kept a few family pets here, like Dane's burro and a couple horses for trail rides. She walked to the stall holding her old cream-colored pony. "Here, Butterball."

The elderly equine shuffled over to her and bumped her hand with his muzzle. She gave him a good scratching and slipped him a small carrot from her pocket. "Now go to bed, honey."

Adam stopped behind her. "Are you talking to me or the horse?"

She turned to face him. "If I were talking to you, I would have said, '*Come* to bed, honey.'"

"Oh, I will." He grabbed her butt and lazily swiveled his growing erection into the cradle of her hips. "I'll come anywhere with you."

She smiled in anticipation. "All set." Climbing the stairs leading to the dark hayloft, she purposely threw some extra twitch into her hips.

A big pair of hands grabbed her butt and made her squeal. "Get that cute ass upstairs before your pony gets an eyeful."

"Adam." She turned to scold him but he hustled her into the hayloft, his hands teasing her breasts and sliding along the increasingly hot and damp center seam of her jeans. "Watch out for the hay chute on the other side. You don't want to fall through it."

A good-sized pile of hay overflowed one corner of the hayloft. Bridget tossed the blanket on the springy yellow-green fodder. Moonlight streamed in through the open door nearby. "Ready for a roll in the hay, Adam?"

"The classic naughty farm-girl fantasy. And you even have the jeans and plaid shirt to match." He traced the line of her jaw to the base of her throat and kissed her. She eagerly responded, wrapping her arms around his neck and welcoming his lips. He sucked and nibbled on her lower lip, running his tongue over her mouth's sensitive points. Their breathing grew more heated. She gently pushed him away and unbuttoned her blue plaid flannel shirt to reveal an old Green Bay Packers T-shirt underneath.

"Can I help?"

"You can help by taking off your shirt like you're outside and working hard."

They both stripped off their shirts a few feet apart, Adam's dark gaze never leaving hers. Bridget unfastened her bra, shivering as the cool night air instantly tightened her nipples.

"Cold?" His sexy voice made her even harder.

"Don't worry, I'll warm up soon."

"Yeah, you will," he promised.

She pulled her flannel shirt on and knotted it under her bare breasts. Her nipples pressed on the soft flannel, though not as soft as Adam's tongue. Her shoes and jeans soon hit the hayloft floor, leaving her in nothing but a lavender thong and the shirt.

"Have mercy." Even in the darkness, the large bulge behind his fly was obvious. "Pinch me, I must be dreaming."

Bridget grinned in satisfaction. "No, I'm the exhausted farm girl innocently taking a nap in the hay after a long day." She reclined on the blanket, making sure her arms boosted her breasts into nice cleavage.

"Who am I? The lusty farmhand who finds her?"

"And after years of longing from afar, his desires overcome his judgment and he awakens her with a kiss." She closed her eyes.

"Hmphh. More like real life." Instead of elaborating on that, he knelt next to her. She stretched, the sweet scent of hay perfuming the air.

"Oh, baby." He knelt between her thighs and skimmed the sides of her body, lingering on her bare hips and the curves of her breasts. She arched into his hands, his big thumbs caressing her nipples through the flannel. He dipped his hands inside the open placket and covered her breasts. She groaned. If only they had a condom, she would have asked him to bend her over a hay bale and take her right then. She pressed her legs together as her clitoris throbbed fiercely.

He dragged his tongue to her navel and stopped. Even in the dim light, his dark eyes sparkled mischievously. "Didn't you say the lusty farmhand wakes you with a kiss?"

"Yes, but—"

"You didn't say where." He pressed a kiss square on the front of her thong, and she squirmed, his hot breath penetrating the lace as if she were naked.

"Oh, yes, *there*." She sighed, her knees falling open.

He pulled her thong to the side and inhaled deeply. "Mmm, I wonder how you taste today, Bridget. Every time it's a little bit different."

He laughed softly and delicately flicked his tongue over her clit, with featherlight touches that had her clutching at the blanket. He pleasured her thoroughly. When she tried to close her thighs because it was so intense, he braced them open with his hands, stroking the tender skin where her thighs met her bottom.

"Salty-sweet, like the time I took a sip of your margarita when we went out for dinner. And I think your cup is overflowing." He darted his tongue deep into her passage.

She quivered under his mouth but he held her tight and alternately licked and sucked her innermost flesh. Every sensation she was experiencing must have shown in her face. She caught him looking at her, his eyes crinkled in appreciation.

"Undo your shirt. I want to see you play with your tits while I play with your hot little pussy."

"Adam," she scolded, "such language."

He sampled her juices again and grinned in satisfaction. "Why did you just get a lot wetter?"

She wanted to deny it but couldn't. Those naughty words coming from his mouth were always a turn-on. She fumbled at the flannel knot and finally undid it, her breasts two pale globes in the starlight. She licked her finger and drew a wet circle around each nipple.

"That's it." He grinned at her and immediately positioned himself between her thighs, as if he was dying to eat her up. His finding pleasure at the very core of her sexuality spurred her on as she caressed and gently pinched her nipples, pretending her hands were his.

He slipped a finger inside her and she clenched around him. He added another finger, his mouth alternating a series of maddening licks and sucks.

Her body burned as she thrashed back and forth, hot enough to practically ignite the hay under her. She dropped her hands away from her breasts, too dazed to continue touching herself.

"Close?" he murmured.

She couldn't speak, only nodded frantically.

"Good." Incredibly, a third finger filled her and she gripped her breast hard.

The climax blasted through her like lightning, zigzagging from her chest to his mouth and fingers, and had her screaming his name so loud she startled the animals below and several mourning doves roosting in the rafters.

He continued mercilessly, lapping up every drop of her wetness. She tried tugging him away but he caught her wrists and pinned them to her belly. "You're not done yet."

She was his sensual captive, his shoulders wedging her legs wide for his feast. He drove her to a second orgasm nearly as powerful as the first, her clit and vagina pulsing frantically under his masterful touch. Her whole body tingled as he gave one last, long, luxurious lick trailing from her clit to swirl around each nipple. Breathless and sated, she could say nothing except, "Adam, that was…"

He pushed a damp curl from her forehead. "I like making you feel good."

He stood and quickly undid his belt buckle and zipper, shoving down his jeans and briefs. He returned to her, on his knees. "Touch me now, sweetheart, before I explode."

She stroked him gently, admiring how his breadth and length filled her palm. His taut head was dripping. She slicked the moisture around the tip as he moaned in satisfaction.

His breath came harder. "Oh, yeah. Faster." She twisted her hand around his cock and he strained into her embrace. "Wish I had a condom. Want to be in you. Feeling you tight around me. Deep."

She shook her head in regret. They couldn't take the chance. Unless…

She let go of him and lay on the blanket.

"No, Bridget, we can't."

She cupped her breasts. "Here."

His jaw fell open. "You want me to do it there?" Despite his shock, his erection tipped even higher.

"I know you like my breasts. Now your cock gets a turn." She fought back a nervous giggle. She'd never done this before with her former boyfriends despite their urging. Adam would understand what a big deal this was for her.

"If you're sure." He bent down and tenderly kissed each nipple.

"Positive." She scooted down a bit so he straddled her waist.

He balanced carefully so as not to rest his full weight on her. "Push them together." She crossed her arms under her breasts and he groaned as he thrust his cock between them. "Oh, Bridget, you are so soft. I could stay here forever."

His penis was hot and hard on her skin, his testicles heavy. He leaned forward to brace his arms over her head. She stretched her fingertips to caress his six-pack abs and his breath hissed. "Sweetheart, this is amazing."

His cock slipped higher on her body, leaving room for her to cup his balls. He jerked violently and froze, muttering numbers under his breath.

"What are you saying?" She'd heard of guys reciting baseball stats to control their orgasms, but Adam wasn't a baseball fan.

"Reciting soybean prices so I don't explode all over you right now."

She burst into laughter, making her breasts jiggle along his length.

"Bridget," he gasped between thrusts, "can't take much more."

"I think you can." She pushed her breasts even higher so their peaks moved through the soft black hair on his belly. The delicious sensations made her shudder in delight despite her two previous orgasms.

Sweat dampened Adam's chest, just like he appeared in her farmhand fantasy. "Bridget, stop me now if you don't want me to finish like this. We've never done this before, this is pretty raw…."

"Don't you want to come all over me, mark me as your own?"

"Oh, yesss…" His breath hissed out. "Mine, all mine."

"Do it." She squeezed his balls hard enough to trigger his climax.

He came, shouting her name, his seed on her breasts and neck. The slick wetness spurred him into a frenzy. She gripped the base of his cock and he came again, groaning and pulsing until his arms shook with fatigue.

She kissed his chest, his scent rising to mix with the equally earthy hay. He slid off to lie at her side, one muscular arm thrown over his head.

A few moments later, he propped himself on one elbow, his smile turned to concern. "Oh, Bridget, I'm so sorry. Let me clean you off." He reached for his discarded shirt, but she stopped him.

"Wait." Giving into some decadent impulse, she

massaged his seed all over her breasts and nipples like some hot, exotic lotion. He had had one of his longest orgasms ever, and she had plenty to rub into her skin.

He stared at her in amazement, his cock jerking against her hip.

She deliberately brought a damp finger to her lips and licked it clean. He gulped. "Delicious. Sweet and salty," she informed him, mimicking his earlier words. She sank back against the blanket, enjoying her skin's tight shininess under the moonlight.

"That—" he paused to catch his breath "—is the sexiest thing I have *ever* seen. I would come again right now if I could."

She laughed until she saw the devilish gleam in his eyes.

"But I bet you can come again right now."

Before she could protest, he rolled onto his back and pulled her into a sitting position on his chest, where his hair tickled her sensitive folds. "Scoot up."

"What?"

"Onto my face."

It was her turn to gasp in shock. Shock mixed with definite arousal.

"You know you want to. I just felt your wetness on my skin." He slowly licked his lips. "Come on up."

"Well, if you insist." She put her knees on either

side of his head, closing her eyes as he spread her open.

"I do." He cupped her butt and snuggled her in tight.

She surrendered herself to his wicked tongue and lips. "Well, ride 'em, cowgirl!"

BRIDGET WAS WEEDING the snap peas in the vegetable garden Monday morning when her parents' pickup pulled in. They climbed down, looking tired and older than their years. Adam came out from the milking parlor to greet them, earning a handshake from her dad and a hug from her mother. The guys headed into the milking parlor as Bridget met her mother in the gravel driveway.

"Hi, Mom, glad you're back." Bridget hugged her mother, who gave her a wan smile.

"That niece and nephew of yours wore me out. It's like herding chickens trying to get them to do anything." Mom climbed the porch steps into the kitchen. "Can I fix you something to eat?"

"No, Mom, you just got home. Sit for a minute." Bridget shooed her into her recliner with a cool drink after a few minutes of halfhearted protests. "Dad checking on the cows?"

Her mother closed her eyes as she rested her head on the chair's lace doily. "Of course. How did it go for you and Adam?"

Bridget froze for a second and then realized her mother meant the farming part. "We got all the milking done pretty much on schedule. Adam and I managed fine on our own, but I think he was surprised at how much work it was." That was an understatement. Regular gym workouts didn't help prepare city muscles for farm work. Her own muscles were killing her, despite the fact Adam had done most of the heavy lifting.

"Does the boy still want to dairy farm?"

Bridget shrugged. "I doubt it. He needs to do something different than futures trading, but I don't know if farming's for him."

Her mother opened her eyes and gave her a steady stare. "Your dad and I might like to do some traveling in a few years. Buy an RV and tour the country. Maybe even Florida for the winter."

"Oh. Sure." Somehow, Bridget hadn't imagined her parents retiring. Sure, Jenna's had, but Jenna was an only child and Colin had taken over the farm. "Dane's too busy traveling with his financial-consulting job, so what would you do? Lease it?"

"That's one option."

"You wouldn't sell it, would you?" Her stomach jumped. The farm had been in their family for more than a hundred years.

"Adam might be interested. Especially if he had a wife who'd grown up in dairying."

Whoa. No. No. Alarm bells as loud as the iron triangle on the back porch rang in her head. "He's not going to find anyone like that living in Chicago."

Her mother gave her a sly smile. "You never know."

"No, I *do* know. Stop smiling at me like that. I just moved away— I'm not moving back, and there's nothing between me and Adam Hale."

"Did I hear my name?" Adam had come in from the milking parlor.

Bridget shot a warning look at her mom. "I was saying it's almost time for us to leave for the city. I have a bunch of things I need to do before tomorrow, and Adam does, too."

"Um, yeah." He took his cap off and ran his fingers through his ungelled hair. He wore a red flannel shirt over faded jeans and looked every inch the young, handsome farmer. If more guys like him had been in her high school's Future Farmers of America chapter, she might have stuck with agriculture instead of switching to sewing. She never figured she'd have to choose between the two again.

Adam gave her a questioning look. "You want to head back now, Bridget?"

"Definitely." She regretted lying to her mom and then to Adam about what she and her mom had been talking about, but the cords of home were twisting her tighter and tighter like fresh-cut hay in a baler. Pretty soon she'd be a solid mass being nibbled to death by cows. "Mom, I'm all packed, and there's a roast in the oven for you and Dad. It should be ready in a couple hours."

Mom struggled to her feet, Adam helping her. She patted his cheek. "Thank you for helping us this weekend. You're a lovely boy, and we're all very proud of you."

Bridget fought back tears at her mother's kind words, knowing he'd had too little tenderness in his life. Adam was doing the same, swallowing hard. "Thank you. That means a lot to me."

Mom nodded. "Nothing but the truth. Now go hop in the shower before you go. Fancy-pants Bridget here might complain about the farm smell in the car."

Bridget groaned. Tender moment over.

He winked at them. "I'll go stick my head under the pump and be back in two shakes of a lamb's tail." He turned the corner, the steps squeaking under his feet as he went upstairs.

"Bridget." Her mom gave her a stern look. "I think that boy has a crush on you. You'd be foolish to pass him up."

She went to her mom and kissed her on the cheek. "You know I want to focus on my career, and I still might win that lingerie design contest."

Her mother shook her head, pursing her lips. "All your fancy bras and panties, and nobody to wear them for."

BRIDGET AND ADAM straggled into his condo several hours later. Adam dumped their luggage in the living room past the narrow foyer and stretched, his vertebrae popping audibly.

Bridget flopped facedown on his leather couch. Despite taking a couple catnaps on their trip, she was beat. Fortunately she'd finished her schoolwork early, otherwise she'd be running around and shrieking in panic instead of relaxing. "Let's order in Chinese food tonight. I have a craving for some kung pao shrimp and General Tso's chicken."

He rubbed his chin. "I guess I could go for an egg roll and some Mongolian beef, but I'm getting tired of carryout. Why don't we ever cook?"

"Too busy, I guess. Why, what do *you* want to eat?"

He got a dreamy look on his face. "Mmm, your mom's meat loaf. That big ham with the brown-sugar glaze and those homemade scalloped potatoes. Maybe a pork roast with potato pancakes and homemade applesauce."

"Does sound good," she agreed. "You know how to cook any of that?" Maybe he'd learned after college because back then, he'd lived on canned spaghetti and leftovers her brother had smuggled from the dining hall.

"No, but you must know all her recipes. Why don't we run to the grocery store and get a ham and some potatoes?"

What was he, crazy? "Adam, my finals start soon, and those scalloped potatoes from scratch take at least a half hour to peel, slice and layer, plus another hour and a half to bake, and the ham takes at least as long."

"You could teach me," he suggested, looking hopeful that she would abandon her nap and anything else she had to do to slave over a huge meal. Next thing she knew, he'd ask her to bake her mother's famous chicken potpie with the ten-ingredient filling and hand-rolled piecrust.

"It would take even longer if I had to explain everything to you." She rolled over and sat up. "What's wrong with ordering Chinese food? We didn't eat any while we were in Wisconsin."

"Yeah, we ate real food in Wisconsin. Family food," he groused.

"Well, learn how to cook real family food, and you're all set," she snapped back. "Do you want Chinese or not?"

"If that's the best you can do." He stomped into the kitchen and riffled through the carryout menus on the fridge.

"Me? Since when am I in charge of meal planning? You fed yourself long before I ever came along."

He reached for the phone to order their food and pushed a button. "Hold on, let me get that voice mail." After listening to the message, he tossed the phone to her. "You better listen to that."

"Hello, Adam, it's Helen Weiss. Just making sure you and Bridget had a safe trip. Bridget, if you're there, call me to let me know how your trip was, and don't stay up *too* late. Love you both."

Well. Her mom couldn't have made her approval of a potential relationship more blatantly obvious. And Bridget thought they'd been so slick this weekend.

"I told you your mom was one sharp cookie, Bridge." He echoed what she was thinking, making it even more irritating.

"It's Bridget, all right?"

"Hey, I only called you that because we had been pretending—and not very well, obviously—that we were just friends. Don't bite my head off if your mom noticed those longing glances you threw my way."

"What are you talking about? You were the one who couldn't keep his eyes off my ass all weekend."

"So sue me! You have a great ass and I loved having it on my face in the hayloft!"

"Thank you!" She fought back a giggle. Maybe this little tiff would all blow over and she could eat her carryout, review her contest stuff and screw his brains out before bed.

But then he frowned at her. "Why *don't* we tell your family about us? They like me—it's not as if I'm some loser you picked up in a bar by your friend Sugar's place."

Back to the tiff. "Because if we tell them, my mother will start imagining a big Wisconsin wedding no matter what I protest and I don't want that." Although she'd always wanted to design her own wedding gown, she thrust that image away firmly. "No."

"You don't want that or you don't want me?"

She had to tread carefully here. He was really sensitive to rejection, thanks to his parents. "Of course I want you—but we want different things. You want the white picket fence around a Victorian farmhouse and I want my degree and my career."

"You only have a couple more years in school, then we could move back to Wisconsin and you could telecommute, or do freelance design."

"That's not how it works. I need to make contacts in the industry and find a job. After I graduate, I might not even stay in Chicago."

"What, move to New York?" He gave her a sour look.

She got mad, too. "Or even L.A. I might win that design contest from Richard's on Rodeo, you know."

"Oh, that's right. Ree-shard might whisk you off

to la-la land where you can sew bras for starlets with more boobs than brains."

"Hey! The two are not mutually exclusive, and you know that darn well!"

"And who said I wanted to marry you, anyway, Bridget?" He spread his arms wide. "No ring here."

"Good. I'd say no if you asked." So there. She skipped the urge to stick out her tongue and concentrated on not letting her lips quiver. Sure, she didn't want to get married right now, but if she ever did, it would be to Adam.

Crap. It had always been Adam, hadn't it? The few guys she'd slept with before him had always come up short compared to him, in more ways than one. Her mad crush on him had developed into genuine liking and now into love.

She *did* love him. Did he love her? He loved her family. Was that part of his attraction for her? A ready-made farm family complete with huge pork roasts and homemade desserts?

His stupid phone rang yet again. "Shit, what's a guy gotta do to order some damn Chinese food around here?" He stomped toward the kitchen.

"Probably telemarketers—let the machine get it." She was too confused about realizing that she loved him to think coherently. The answering machine clicked on.

"Hello, darlink, it's Daria." The voice of a woman

who sounded like Natasha from the *Rocky and Bull-winkle* cartoon purred into the condo.

"Telemarketers have bad Russian accents and call you 'darlink'?" Was he playing some kind of game?

"I swear, I told her not to call me. And she's Polish."

He moved toward the phone, but Bridget jumped from the couch and blocked his path, hands on her hips. "Daria—your girlfriend from last fall? Why is she calling you?"

The Natasha sound-alike continued, "So, darlink, is your chubby blond milkmaid still around?"

"What?" Bridget screeched. "How does she know I'm a chubby blond milkmaid?"

"Bridget—" He raised his hands. "I never said a thing about you to her."

"How does she know about me? Have you been dating her, too?" She fought back tears. If he had, he was *gone,* love or no love.

"No, of course not." He looked shocked.

She stuck her finger in his face. "And I am *not* chubby, by the way."

"I never called you chubby!"

The message continued mercilessly, "Call me if she's history. Or even if she's not. Doesn't matter to me. *Ciao,* darlink."

Bridget narrowed her eyes. "*Darlink,* I'm confused. I thought *Daria* was the one who was history."

"She is. She stopped by my office once and saw

your picture there. I blocked her from my cell phone but she must have found out the new home number I had to get for my high-speed Internet hookup."

"What is she, some kind of stalker?"

"She wants to get back together with me, but I told her it's never gonna happen." He stabbed the delete button on the answering machine until it erased her message.

"Why did you split in the first place? Dane said she had a bad temper."

"That was part of it." He set his jaw and crossed his arms over his chest.

"And the other part was?" Good grief, it was like pulling teeth with him to get him to open up sometimes.

"I don't want to discuss it. Can we move on to something else?" He gave her a hard stare she'd never seen before.

"Move on? Am I messing up your meeting agenda? Well, let me tell you, buddy, when you're in Wisconsin staring at some cow's backside, your agenda will fly out the window."

"My agenda? What about *your* agenda? You have this grand plan to become a world famous lingerie designer, and I think that's great. But you won't compromise, you won't bend even the least little bit." He pinched his fingers together so only a sliver of space showed.

"So what are you willing to give up, Adam?

You're not interested in meeting me halfway. You want your awful trading job because it makes you a lot of money despite the risks to your health, you want your dairy farm in Middle of Nowhere, Wisconsin, and you apparently want me there on your farm to cook you potpies and potato pancakes and pork roasts. *Without* marrying me, which as we both know is *not* going to fly with my very large father and two even larger brothers."

He started to argue with her and stopped, knowing darn well she was right.

She blinked hard. "Look, I need a clear head for my finals coming up, not to mention my entry for the contest, and this discussion isn't going to help."

"Fine. What size kung pao shrimp do you want?"

"None. I'm going to my place. I need some breathing room." And room to think about what loving Adam meant to her, and what she would do if they couldn't work things out.

She stood and crossed the living room to pick up her overnight bag, leaving his there. She had enough baggage without taking his on.

ADAM STARED at his computer screen, not seeing the numbers rolling by. He hadn't been sleeping well in the past several days since Bridget had left him. She hadn't called, but to be fair, he hadn't called her, either.

He didn't want to be fair. All of her digs about his inflexibility and ambition had stung. Probably because they were accurate.

He sat back and sighed, rubbing his eyes. He had several weeks' vacation due, but he'd never bothered to put in for any. Maybe he'd e-mail his supervisor and take some time off in June or July. He could rent a lake cabin up north, go fishing or hiking.

By himself, though? That was the big question. He missed Bridget a lot, but she expected too much from him. Dial back on his career while her own was the main focus of her life? Unfair.

Spill his guts about Daria and the most nerve-wracking episode of his life? No way. That was a closed book.

But he made the mistake of looking over at the old picture of Bridget and him from Colin's wedding. Her beautiful face tipped up to his. His expression something between a smile and a grimace trying to control his wayward body at her nearness.

He flipped the frame facedown. Enough mooning over her. There was all the time in the world to let things settle down. After six years, what were a couple more weeks?

A commotion in the cubicles outside caught his attention. He opened his door and stepped into chaos. Someone was flat on the floor, his legs the only visible part as guys crowded around his upper body, cursing and shouting for someone to call 911 and get the defibrillator that was stuck on the office wall.

Adam ran over. It was Tom, pale and sweaty. As Adam watched in horror, Tom's eyes rolled back in his head and his chest stopped heaving.

Erik, a younger trader who ran marathons and obviously knew some first aid, felt for a pulse. "Damn it, who else knows CPR around here?" Erik must have been a Boy Scout since he pulled a small CPR face shield from a pouch on his keychain.

Adam pushed his way through the crowd. He'd been certified since his teen years. "I do."

"Okay, you do chest compressions and I'll do rescue breathing."

Adam dropped into place, laced his fingers and locked his elbows, counting compressions under his breath. He'd never done this on a real person before, and he tried to blank Tom's creaking, cracking rib cage from his mind.

Somebody trotted back with the red defibrillator box, and Erik yanked it open while another guy took over breathing. He slapped the sticky pads on Tom's chest. "Okay, stop."

Adam and the other rescuer sat back on their heels. Adam clenched his fists in impotent anger. How could Tom have been so careless to gamble away his health? For what? Money?

The defibrillator buzzed. Erik shook his head. "It says we need to shock him. Stand back." He pushed a button and the machine whined, then zapped Tom, who jerked like a hooked fish on a dock and stilled. Nothing.

"Again." Erik pushed the button a second time. Tom quivered again.

Adam stared at the digital display. After an agonizingly long pause, wavy heart rhythms trailed across the screen. "I think he's back!"

A loud cheer rose from the huddle of traders. Adam checked to make sure Tom was breathing on his own now. His chest rose and fell, albeit weakly. Adam extended his hand to Erik. "Good job, man."

"You, too, Adam. Too close for my liking." Erik shook his hand and wiped sweat off his forehead. The paramedics ran in at that point and Erik filled them in. They bundled Tom onto a stretcher and told them they were taking him to the big university hospital nearby.

Another colleague, one of Tom's closest friends, hung up a phone, his face sour. "Just spoke with Tom's ex-wife. She said she'd call the hospital later to see how he's doing."

"Nice." Adam shook his head. Not even going over to see if he lived or died? "You should go over now," he told Tom's friend.

"Ah, I'm right in the middle of a trade." He

looked over at his computer. "If I lose money on this, I'm in trouble."

He couldn't be bothered to leave his work to go, either? What kind of place was this? "Screw it. I'm going to the hospital." Adam stomped into his office and turned off the power to his computer, not bothering to shut it down properly. As he was grabbing his jacket, he spotted the photo of Bridget still facedown on his desk.

He picked it up and looked again at her open, trusting face. She trusted him with the good and bad parts of her life. Maybe it was time he trusted her with the same. He slid the frame into his briefcase.

He might not be coming back, and that photo represented the only positive and decent thing in his office. Maybe even his life.

12

"TEN MINUTES to showtime, Bridget." Her instructor, Jennifer, stopped next to where Bridget made a last-minute seam adjustment on Sugar's dress.

Bridget nodded and Jennifer strode to the next student designer. The week since her big fight with Adam had been a bizarre combination of frenetic days and achingly long nights. She had gone to his place to get most of her things when she knew he'd be at work. Neither had made the first move to contact each other. She missed him terribly, not just as her lover, but also as her best friend.

A sudden movement under her needle brought her attention back to her task. "Hold still, Sugar. I don't want to jab you." Her friend was so excited about modeling in the school's annual lingerie fashion show that she was wiggling all over the place. If Bridget got a good grade, she would be able to skip the introductory lingerie design class and jump right into the advanced seminar.

Sugar's costume was a modified version of her

strip-club fairy-queen outfit, only with permanent seams instead of Velcro and a bra and full-coverage panties to go underneath instead of pasties and a thong.

"Sorry, Bridget. This is so exciting!" She clapped her hands together and likely would have jumped up and down if Bridget hadn't cleared her throat in warning.

"Okay, done." Bridget knotted the thread and clipped the ends. "Now you can hop up and down. Go over in the corner and do it. Next!" She beckoned to Jinx, who was sitting in a portable canvas lawn chair.

"I'm cool." She set down a pink highlighter and copy of the *Journal of Victorian Literary Feminism* and stood, her red vinyl bodysuit creaking. "But this isn't like my other suit. The breast cups don't open."

Bridget circled her with a critical eye. "Good. I sewed them shut. This fashion show doesn't need any costume-type stunts."

Jinx grinned. "Fine, Bridget. I'm sure no one would faint at the sight of a nipple, but if that's the way you want it."

"Absolutely. The show guidelines are very clear. Any nudity, accidental or otherwise, counts against my grade."

"Uptight. What's the point of a lingerie collection if you can't see any body parts?"

Bridget pointed at her third model. "Look at Electra's outfit. She's mostly covered but still sexy."

"Thanks, Bridget." Electra patted her Greco-Roman-type curls caught on the back of her head. Bridget had put her in a toga-type tunic that dipped deep between her breasts and draped across her lower back, revealing the two dimples above her bottom.

"With your height and build, you look like a Greek goddess." A lump settled in Bridget's throat. "You all look wonderful. I wish I could describe how much I appreciate you modeling my designs. This is such a big deal for me…." She trailed off. And she had no one to share it with. She'd down-played the show's importance to her family because she knew they wouldn't be able to attend anyway, and as for Adam…well, he knew about the show but she didn't expect him, either.

Sugar handed her a tissue. "Don't cry—you'll ruin your makeup."

Bridget looked at her sheepishly and carefully dabbed at her watery eyes. Electra patted her shoulder and Jinx dug around in her duffel bag. "My offer to whip that jerk's ass still stands. Here it is!" She drew out her red whip and cracked it menacingly.

Bridget burst into laughter, her first time in several days. "Go ahead and walk the runway with that. Just don't put out anyone's eye."

"Since you won't let me show off my ruby nipple rings, it's the least you can do."

The show's director called for places and Bridget gave her models some last-minute advice. "Remember, as you're walking the runway, the clothing stays on. Don't get confused and start taking it off."

The girls laughed and joined the other models. Electra and Sugar in particular stood out among the skinny waifs readying themselves to show their heavily padded assets.

Realizing her creations were in good hands, Bridget sucked in a deep breath and fluffed her curls. Her white wrap blouse needed a final straightening over her black skirt and she quickly tied on a blue silk sash. Her hands slowed as she realized she'd made the sash from the leftover fabric used for her cocktail dress for Sugar's party. Something old made into something new, not borrowed but definitely blue.

She was going to be blue if she didn't stop mooning over Adam. Giving the material one last caress, she firmly put him out of her mind and hurried to the wings where she could peek at her friends.

ADAM GRIPPED the bouquet of flowers, hoping his sweaty hands didn't wilt them. This was the second time he'd bought flowers this week. The first were for Tom, who was slowly recovering in the cardiac care unit a few blocks away.

That could have been *him* lying dead on the office floor. He looked out the cab window and shivered despite the warm May weather. What had Tom wished for when the first pains gripped his chest? Family, happiness, *love?* Not more time at work, that was for damn sure.

Only a short distance from the historic department store that was hosting Bridget's fashion show, traffic was in gridlock. "I'll stop here." He paid the cab-driver and hopped onto State Street, a busy shopping area close to the popular Millennium Park that over-looked Lake Michigan.

The street was crowded with the usual mix of tourists and uptight business types trying to get around the tourists. *Like him,* he noted wryly as he dodged map-readers and photo-takers.

He double-checked his watch. Ten minutes to showtime. He pushed through the revolving door into the air-conditioned department store, a welcome relief from the mugginess outside. He wouldn't be surprised if thunderstorms hit the city later.

Hopefully his own evening wouldn't be stormy. He took the escalator upstairs to the show, buttoned his best suit jacket and straightened his hideously ex-pensive blue silk tie, the one he'd bought with his first trading paycheck back when his money burnt a hole in his pocket.

He stepped into the show and found a corner to

stand in where he had full view of the runway, but wasn't blocking the various TV cameras and print media photographers in the back of the room. The first model teetered along in some yellow dress that looked like it had been run over and shredded by a combine. Definitely not Bridget's. He eyed a couple more models impatiently until a familiar face stepped onto the runway. There was no mistaking Sugar Jones, Frisky's number-one Kitten, for anyone else. She worked that tiny glittery negligee, flipping the floaty hem and twirling in time to the heavy rock beat.

Even to his inexperienced gaze, Sugar *owned* that runway, and the crowd's rising murmurs confirmed it. He grinned. Sugar was mentally on stage at Frisky's even if she was mostly clothed. Her round of applause was definitely bigger than the previous girls'.

Throughout the show, he recognized Bridget's other dancer friends, Jinx and Electra. That Jinx, cracking her red whip, drawing a shocked gasp from the audience followed by loud clapping. He shook his head. He bet she'd still like to use it on him for upsetting Bridget.

Although he tried several times, he couldn't spot Bridget anywhere. She was probably backstage, helping her friends into their other outfits.

For their big finale, all the models walked the runway and the tuxedoed emcee called the designers to take their curtain call. Adam's heart pounded hard as he saw Bridget for the first time in six long days. Her cheeks were flushed and her eyes sparkled as she took her bow.

Adam shoved the bouquet under his arm and clapped furiously for her, the woman who had worked so hard to come to Chicago and do what she loved best. He shoved his fingers in his mouth and gave a piercing whistle, not caring if it was tacky.

The emcee quieted the crowd and gestured to a tiny brunette dressed all in black. "Thank you all for coming to our annual fashion show. Before you leave, Jennifer Miller, the show's coordinator, has a special announcement to make."

The coordinator took the microphone. "Thank you. I have an important guest with me this evening." She gestured to a blond man who had come onstage. "Richard from the famous Richard's on Rodeo has come here from Beverly Hills to make two very special announcements."

Holy crap, that was Ree-shard himself, the guy whose contest Bridget was a finalist in? What if she won? He might lose her to Rodeo Drive. If he hadn't lost her already.

BRIDGET'S JAW DROPPED. Richard was here? Did that mean she'd won his contest? Her knees shook so hard she was afraid she'd fall over.

Richard took the microphone and grinned, his white teeth shining almost as brightly as the stage spotlights. "As always, I'm thrilled to be here in Chicago." He spoke with a slight French accent, emphasizing the last syllable of "Chicago." He went on about his plans to expand into a boutique space affiliated with the department store they stood in, but Bridget didn't catch many details since her heart was pounding so hard.

Richard stopped yakking and peered over at the group of designers. "And by a happy coincidence, the winner of my nationwide lingerie design contest is here in Chicago, as well. Ten thousand dollars and an exclusive contract with Richard's on Rodeo goes to Bridget Weiss!"

She couldn't speak. All the air was knocked from her lungs, which wasn't helped by a smothering group hug from Sugar, Electra and Jinx.

Richard managed to fight his way through the female flesh surrounding her and took her hand to lead her down the runway. At the very end, he kissed her on both cheeks, Gallic-style, and hugged her as he muttered, "Don't go fainting on me, okay?" in a very non-Gallic accent.

She nodded in surprise and blinked away tears of excitement. A ripple in the crowd below caught her eye as a black-haired man pushed his way to the runway.

Adam.

He looked up at her, his face serious. Their gazes met and meshed. Richard, the crowd and all the noise fell away, leaving only the two of them. He lifted a huge bouquet of gorgeous blue Dutch irises and white lily of the valley, their perfume rising to her nose. She knelt and held his strong wrist instead of the flowers.

"Bridget." His beautiful lips formed her name.

"Adam." Her eyes filled with tears again.

He smiled at her. "Enjoy your triumph. We'll talk later."

Richard put his hand on her shoulder. "He's right, darling. Take the flowers now, talk later."

She reluctantly released Adam and accepted the bouquet. Richard led her up the runway, away from Adam. Just once, she looked over her shoulder to see him clapping for her. As a designer, she had her prize, but she still had to fight for the biggest prize of all: Adam's love.

MORE THAN AN HOUR LATER, Bridget's face hurt from all the smiling. She finally had a second to herself backstage to admire Adam's flowers. Thanks to her gardening, she knew blue irises stood for faith and hope and lily of the valley meant return of happiness. She could do with some of that. Suddenly, she felt his presence behind her and turned.

"Congratulations, Bridget." He shoved his hands

into the pockets of his lovely suit, the shirt's pure whiteness emphasizing his stunning dark coloring.

"Thank you, Adam." There was an awkward pause as neither knew what to do next, but Bridget decided to hell with it and held out her arms for a hug. Even if their future as lovers was uncertain, she hoped their friendship was not.

He tentatively took her in his arms. She pressed her face into his suit jacket and inhaled his wonderful spicy scent. Tension drained from her and he pressed the lightest of kisses on the top of her head.

She would have been happy to stand there all day in his embrace, but the bouquet slipped from her grasp and fell. "The flowers!"

He bent and handed them to her for the second time that evening. "Not even bruised."

Unlike her heart, which had only starting beating again at the sight of him. "Oh, Adam, I can't believe you came."

"Sure, I came." He checked out the backstage area, which looked as if a fashion tornado had rolled through. "Where are your parents?"

"Wisconsin." Rats. He was too sharp not to notice their absence.

"What? They didn't come? I can't imagine them missing your important occasion, farm or no."

She didn't meet his gaze. "I didn't invite them because I knew they were too busy."

"Did they tell you that?" He lifted her chin with one finger.

"No, but I know how things are." She shrugged. "And the whole lingerie thing would have embarrassed them."

"Give them a chance, Bridget. You never know, they might come around. And I would do anything for you."

Her jaw fell open. He'd never said anything like that before.

"Bridget," Jennifer called to her, with Richard in tow. Bridget bit back a shriek of frustration. Just when she thought they were getting somewhere. Jennifer hugged her. "Did I tell you or did I tell you that I have the eye? I was right!"

"Yes, you were right, Jennifer," Bridget reassured her. She was still keenly aware of Adam's presence behind her.

Apparently so was Richard. "Aren't they adorable together!" he exclaimed. "Oh, Jennifer, they match! Did you plan your outfits?"

Match? Bridget looked at Adam in surprise. They both had white shirts, he in a black suit and she in her black skirt, but the surprising thing was that her blue silk sash exactly matched his tie.

Adam shrugged his broad shoulders. "I like this shade of blue because Bridget looks beautiful in her dress of this color."

She gave a little sigh and almost kissed him.

Richard gave a matching sigh and fanned himself. "How *sweet*. Isn't that absolutely *adorable*, Jennifer?"

Jennifer pinched his forearm, earning an indignant squawk. "Cut the camp, Ricky, or I'll let everyone know we grew up together in Peoria. By the way, Bridget, Ricky picked your designs to win all on his own. Friendship doesn't come into play when he's giving away a design contract and ten grand. Right, Ricky?"

"Damn straight. And it's Ree-shard, remember?" he muttered. "We're in public. Anyway, Bridget!" He resumed his flamboyant French accent. "How clever your designs are! Especially for our clients. They get the surgical endowments, shall we say? And they come to my boutique. 'Oh, Richard, my back hurts.' 'Oh, Richard, I am starting to sag. Help me, Richard.' What do they expect with a hundred-pound body and ten-pound breasts?"

"They expect miracles from you, Richard. Expensive miracles." Jennifer grinned at her friend.

"Exactement." He smiled smugly at her. "And with Bridget's new bras, they will get their expensive miracle. Of course we will discuss money matters later."

"In addition to the money matters, I have a few ideas of my own." It was risky, but what did Bridget have to lose? "I want my designs to debut under their own line and we can call it Brigitte." If Ricky could become Ree-shard, Bridget could become Brih-zheet, like she'd joked about with Adam at the farm.

"Your own line, named after you?" Richard folded his arms across his chest.

"Exclusive to your store," she reminded him. "Like Brigitte Bardot."

His perfectly groomed blond eyebrows flew up. "Our ad agency would *love* that. Maybe we could get permission to use her likeness."

Jennifer nodded approvingly, so Bridget forged ahead with the most important thing. "And I want to work from Chicago so I can finish my education. Jennifer says you have other designers who telecommute."

"Yes, yes, I do. Jennifer." He swatted her arm. "You didn't *tell* me Bridget was going to be such a tough negotiator. Although I can clearly see why she wants to stay in Chicago." He eyeballed Adam, who took it like a sport, having plenty of practice thanks to her dancer friends.

Adam shook his head. "It's Bridget's decision where she moves."

What did that mean? How could he move anywhere with her, given his trading job and farming plans? But now wasn't the time for that discussion. "I want to finish my bachelor's degree here." She at least knew that for sure.

"Oh, yes, who wants all that nasty Southern California sun and sea when you can have Chicago snow and sleet?" Richard waved his hand back and forth. "Anyhow, I have your address, and I'll have my assistant messenger the contract Monday. I'll be at the Palmer House Hilton until Wednesday."

"Sounds great." Now that she knew Richard hadn't shot down her proposals, relief rushed over her. She cheek-kissed him and hugged Jennifer before the Peoria pair pranced off to Richard's adoring public.

Then she and Adam were alone. She took a deep breath and faced him. "Wow." She gave a nervous laugh.

"Wow, indeed." He gestured at the bouquet. "Do you, um, like the flowers?"

"They're wonderful." She ran her finger along the yellow stripe on the blue iris petals and flicked a white bell-like bloom of lily of the valley.

"I asked the florist to put together a spring bouquet to win back a woman I'd been foolish enough to let go." He stroked her cheek. "Is it working?"

She held his hand against her face. "Yes. Now let's go home."

13

"JUST SLIP IT IN, ADAM." Bridget's husky instructions didn't help his nervous hands any. He fumbled the keys to his condo before unlocking the door.

"What a storm!" She followed him into his apartment and stood to the side as he pulled her fashion-show suitcases into his foyer. She wore his black jacket over her blouse, which had been drenched as they left the department store. Being somewhat a gentleman and mostly the possessive type, he'd immediately offered her his jacket to wear home.

"Here's your suit coat." She peeled it off and handed it to him. The transparent white fabric revealed her thin lace bra and mouthwateringly plump breasts. "Sorry if it's a bit damp."

"That's fine." He tossed the jacket on the armchair. He had to clear the air. "Come sit."

He tugged her to sit next to him on the couch, determined to tell her the whole story. "Bridget, I want to say that I am so proud of you for winning that award tonight."

"Thanks, Adam." She hugged herself in glee.

"Do you really want to stay in Chicago? I'm sure there are plenty of design schools in L.A. if you wanted to work on-site at Richard's on Rodeo."

"Are you trying to get rid of me, Adam?" She narrowed her eyes. "If you're getting back together with that Daria chick, you need to tell me now."

"No, it's not Daria. Well, it is, but not what you think," he said hastily. "Listen, I'm botching this royally. I get around you and I can't think straight," he complained.

"Try hard, Adam. Try *really* hard."

"Okay, about Daria." He took a deep breath. "She was a model and traveled a lot. On her last trip before we broke up, I knew when she was returning and went over to her place to welcome her home. We'd had a fight before she left, and I wanted to surprise her, so I waited in her lobby."

"You weren't planning on breaking up with her?"

"No, not until I saw the limo pull up to the curb and she got out with this old guy, bald as an egg, wrinkles, the whole bit. I thought she'd shared a ride from the airport, but she kissed him. I mean *really* kissed him, like he was her boyfriend."

Bridget grimaced but he continued. "I burst out the lobby doors. Her back was to me, so she thanked him for buying the fur coat she was wearing and how she'd had such a lovely time in the Virgin

Islands with him." How grossly inappropriate a place for them.

"So she'd gone on vacation with that geezer? And he bought her a fur? He wasn't a family friend, was he?"

Sweet Bridget, trying to put the best spin on it, even for a girl she disliked. "Nope, Daria's family moved back to Poland a few years ago. I said something like, 'What the hell's going on here?' and the old guy took one look at my face and hopped in the limo. She followed and they screeched off. Later she admitted that most of her so-called modeling trips had been vacations with big-time spenders."

She hopped off the couch and paced his living room. "How could she do this to you? You, of all people. You are good and kind and—"

"Stop, Bridget." He stood and caught her elbows.

"What about your girlfriend after Daria? Did you tell her all this?"

He finally smiled at her concerned face. "I just did."

"Me? You didn't date anyone from last fall until you found me at Frisky's?"

"Nope. I took a temporary vow of celibacy."

"Really?"

"Is that so hard to believe?"

"Well, yes, it is. Colin and Dane have always complained that you were the one getting all the girls…even two at a time."

His jaw dropped. "A threesome? I never did that."

"Not even with a couple cheerleaders in college?"

He cast his mind back. "Are those goofballs still talking about that? I was dating a cheerleader and her roommate was drunk. I carried the roommate home, my girlfriend put her to bed—alone—and my girlfriend and I… Well, I was a typical twenty-year-old. It wasn't like we were in the same room."

"Oh." Surprisingly, her face fell. "That's all it was?"

"Disappointed?" He ran his hands to her shoulders. "Don't be. Once Daria dropped her little fur-covered bombshell, I had a lot of time to think about my past relationships and I didn't like the conclusions I came to." His ears grew hot from embarrassment, but he gamely continued. "I realized I was skimming along, not caring to look beneath the surface of the women I dated and not wanting to reveal much about myself. If someone wanted to get to know me better, meet my family—"

She made a comical face. "*That* would have gotten rid of any of them."

He laughed. "See, you already know the worst about my family. And the worst about me and my shallow, selfish past."

"After all that dough you dropped to bail your parents out, I dare anybody to call you selfish." She moved closer. "Whatever bad judgment you've shown in the past, I think you've redeemed yourself.

After all, you had the good taste to go out with *me*."
Despite her confident words, doubt shaded her eyes.

"If you'll still have me, Bridget." He traced the porcelain-smooth skin of her jaw. "I missed you like crazy this past week, and I want to be with you."

"I want to be with you, too." She threw her arms around his neck and kissed him. He kissed her back and meant it, her pliant lips opening under his eager tongue. Her mouth was tangy from the champagne they'd served at the fashion show, but the little bubbles rising in his blood were from her closeness.

He pushed all questions of family, education and careers to the back of his mind and focused on showing her how he felt. "Oh, baby. You are so damn sexy." He immediately hardened as she undid her blouse. She wore a sheer pale-pink bra almost the exact shade of her nipples, those delicate peaks begging to be sucked on.

So he did just that, dropping to his knees on the rug and taking one into his mouth through the fabric. She gasped and grabbed his hair while he cupped her other breast and thumbed its peak. She made sexy moans in the back of her throat.

He moved to her other nipple, but the fabric was starting to get in his way. Too impatient to wait for her to undress, he dragged her blouse and bra straps off her shoulders, baring her breasts.

She shifted a bit, her elbows pinned to her side by

the clothing, which of course had the advantage of pushing her breasts together.

"Leave it. You're hog-tied, like on the farm."

"Adam, you goof, nobody hog-ties dairy cattle." She shook her head, making all that pale flesh jiggle.

"Don't care," he managed to say before pleasuring her again. She squealed as he gave one ripe nipple a long, sensuous lick before sucking it deep. He loved her intense responsiveness to his mouth and touch.

"Adam, please." She wiggled her luscious bottom at him. "Make love to me now."

He raised his head briefly, ignoring the pounding throb of his cock. This was all for her. Well, not all for her—he was enjoying it, too. "I thought I was." He gently squeezed a plump breast, circling his finger around the cotton-candy-pink tip. Under his fascinated glance, its color darkened to a deeper strawberry hue. Hmm, that usually only happened when she was almost ready. He hoped he wouldn't be overly ready himself.

Replacing his finger with his tongue, he hazarded a nip with his teeth and was rewarded with a total body shudder from her. He nipped harder and her knees wobbled.

He wrapped his arms around her hips to brace her but was relentless with his mouth and tongue, switching from breast to breast as her trembling grew stronger. Her sweet scent of arousal rose to his nose, warm and musky. *That* was next.

Her hips thrust against his chest. "Oh, you're making me—ah!" She gave a short scream and her back stiffened as she climaxed. She gave a longer scream, ending with his name drawn out in a long sob, which was music to his ears.

He caught her as her knees buckled and eased her next to him on the rug, her pale skin reddened with a bright orgasmic hue. Her breathing slowed as he fought the urge to drag up her skirt and dive between her thighs. "Wow, sweetheart, you've never come like that before."

She gave him a lopsided grin. "It *has* been a week since we made love, Adam. I was a little worked up."

"And now?" He sure hoped she was still worked up, because he was in a big way.

She shucked off her blouse and bra. "That was a very nice appetizer, but I'd like the main course now." Lying on the rug, she hitched her skirt up to show her pink lace garter belt and black stockings framing a tiny pink thong.

His jaw dropped as she lifted one boot-clad leg into the air and ran her hand down her thigh.

She gave him a sly smile. "Show me how hungry you are."

THE DOORBELL RANG. Adam pried open his eyes and glared at his nightstand clock. 1:00 a.m., and he and Bridget had just fallen asleep after round two or three. If it was Daria, he was calling the cops. He groaned and rolled out of bed. Bridget murmured, still sound asleep, and he pulled the sheet over her naked body.

Throwing on some pajama bottoms and his robe, he staggered down the hall and into the foyer, tripping over the umbrella he'd left to dry.

He crashed into the wall, rattling the pictures and almost toppling the coatrack. "Ow, damn!"

"Adam? That you, buddy?"

He jammed his eye against the peephole, the pain in his knee shoved aside by panic. Bridget's brother Dane, big, blond and soaking wet.

"Adam, it's Dane. Open the door."

What to do, what to do? Dane knew he was home thanks to his knocking everything around and would be insulted if he didn't let him in. Another panicky thought hit. Had Dane and Colin learned about him and Bridget? Driving from Wisconsin to kick his ass would be right up their alley.

Well, Bridget was their sister, and maybe he did warrant an ass-kicking for sneaking around and making love to her in every way imaginable. Maybe this was a sign to call it quits—let her find some other guy who deserved her more.

He took a deep breath and opened the door. Dane broke into a grin. "Adam. Am I glad to see you."

Okay, no ass-kicking. Yet.

Dane stepped into the front hall, water beaded on his black trench coat and luggage. Luggage?

"Oh, what a night! I was only supposed to have a quick layover at O'Hare on my way to meeting a client in New York, but they canceled my flight because of the thunderstorms here and the tornado warning south of the city." Dane hung his coat on the rack and ran his hands though his wet hair. "Some jerk stole my umbrella at the airport, and there are no hotel rooms at all."

"Sounds like quite a night," Adam said weakly.

"Sorry to barge in on you, man. I tried calling Bridget but she wasn't home. I tried you about an hour ago, but there was no answer."

He vaguely remembered the phone ringing when they were making love. He hadn't answered it, naturally. "Oh. Yeah. I, um, couldn't get to the phone and forgot to check my messages."

"Well, no problem. I'm glad you were home. Mind if I bunk here until I get another flight?"

Adam knew it was coming and it still horrified him. But there was only one answer he could give. "Sure. No problem."

Fortunately, his office/guest room was on the other side of the living room. Snuggling with Bridget with Dane in the next room was a real mood killer. Adam gathered some bedding and towels for Dane, surreptitiously closing his bedroom door.

He had just about herded Dane into the guest room when his sharp blue eyes spotted Bridget's purse, hastily tossed onto a chair earlier in the evening. "Hey, you have company?" He winked. "No wonder you couldn't answer the phone. If you want me to take off, I can call and see if Bridget's answering her phone yet. Don't know where she could be this time of night." He frowned.

Adam shook his head frantically. "No need to disturb her." He had to switch her cell phone off unless he wanted Dane to hear it ringing ten feet away. "Well, good night, Dane. Get some sleep, and maybe we can go out for coffee tomorrow." He'd need some—after sneaking Bridget home and coming back. Dane always got up at six.

"Thanks again, buddy." Dane smiled and closed the guest-room door. Adam ran to Bridget's purse to turn off her phone.

"Adam?" Bridget stood in the hall, her body clearly outlined under one of his casual shirts. "I thought I heard voices."

"No, it's okay. Go back to bed."

"Is someone here? What's going on?"

"Bridget?" Dane came roaring out of the guest room, bare to the waist.

"Dane?" Her eyes widened. "What are you doing here?"

"What am I doing here?" He clenched his fists,

big biceps and pecs flexing. "Adam, you better explain why my sister is coming out of your bedroom at one in the morning."

Damn it, her brother was built like a bull after growing up on a dairy farm. Adam hoped he wouldn't embarrass himself by crying like a girl when Dane made him feel some serious pain.

Besides, Adam deserved a beating for sneaking around with her. He knew a bunch of street-fighting tricks from his misspent youth, but wouldn't use them on Dane. The three of them stood frozen in their respective tracks, caught in a triangle of shock and shame.

Bridget crossed her arms over her chest, but looked more exasperated than anything. "Yes, Dane, it's exactly what you think. Adam and I are sleeping together."

Adam winced. She *had* to wave a red cape in front of the bull. Dane lowered his head and charged, not for Bridget, but for him.

He barely jumped clear as Dane knocked over a chair. "Dane, look, man, let's all sit down and talk like— Oof!"

Bull-Boy had nailed him right in the solar plexus with his shoulder, knocking the wind out of him. Adam fell back onto the rug, gasping for air as Dane landed on him.

"You son of a bitch! Treating her like one of your bimbo girlfriends."

Dane's bulk on his ribs wasn't helping his breathing problem any. He dimly heard Bridget holler her brother's name. Desperate, he blindly punched at him, connecting with his jaw.

Dane cursed and shifted his weight enough for Adam to get some oxygen. Unfortunately, Dane used the change of angle to pop Adam in the eye.

Damn, that hurt. Now one eye was swelling and the other was watering. Given the low light in the apartment, he could barely see anyway. Dane's shadow loomed over him, looking like he was about to put those ham-hock hands of his around Adam's windpipe and squeeze.

Adam lunged forward, his forehead crashing into Dane's nose. If it came down to avoiding strangulation, old habits of street-fighting died hard.

Bridget's brother rolled off and clutched at his nose. Pissed off now, Adam jumped on Dane and landed knuckle punches to his gut. He doubted they'd leave a mark due to Dane's beefiness, but they were enough to distract Dane from his plan of choking him to death.

Not enough of a distraction. Dane flipped Adam underneath him again and went for the throat. Adam put the heel of his palm under Dane's chin and shoved. Damn it, he wouldn't last another two minutes with his former best friend, and for what? Going after the only girl he'd ever loved?

Love? His eyes widened. He was a freaking idiot to not realize until now that he loved Bridget, as his muscles were trembling with fatigue from wrestling her brother.

Love was going to get him killed.

BRIDGET'S SHRIEKS to knock off this nonsense immediately simply weren't penetrating the angry testosterone fog surrounding those two yahoos.

Where was a good hose when you needed one? That always worked with the barn tomcats. She looked around the room and spotted the vase of flowers Adam had given her.

Bridget grabbed the irises out of the vase and upended it over the two idiots.

They sputtered in surprise. She planted a foot in her brother's ribs and shoved at him until he rolled off Adam.

"Enough!" She set down the vase and put her hands on her hips. "You!" She pointed at Dane. "Beating up my boyfriend. And you." She pointed at said boyfriend. "Barely standing up for yourself, letting him punch you. Col says you're the best dirty fighter he knows. Come on!"

Adam blinked, his eye a swollen red and purple. "I didn't want to hurt him that bad. He might want kids someday."

Dane glared at her, his face flushed and dripping

watery blood. "I'm gonna call Mom and Dad, and then I'm gonna call Colin!"

"Don't you dare call anyone, Dane Herbert Weiss!" Bridget tapped his swollen nose and he hissed in pain.

"Herbert?" Adam asked, struggling to his feet and pulling his robe around him.

"Shut your mouth," Dane told him in a nasally voice.

Bridget kicked him in the thigh, probably doing more harm to her toes than him. "No, you shut your mouth, you tattletale. Mom and Dad will have a heart attack to get a phone call at 2:00 a.m., and Colin has to get up in two hours anyway."

Dane subsided into dire mutterings and stood, flipping his wet hair out of his face. "Come on, Bridget, we're leaving." He beckoned to her imperiously.

"I don't know what 'we' you're referring to. *I* am staying here. You can either stay or leave." She pointed at the front door.

"Stay? No way in hell I'm staying here. I'd rather sleep on a park bench than remain under his roof after knowing what he's done."

"What exactly have I done, Dane?" Adam frowned. "Did I date your sister when she was fresh out of high school? Did I ever treat her inappropriately when we met at your family functions? Did I even hint that I might have strong feelings for her, or did I cover them up for *years* until she came to me?"

"You did?" Dane's fists unclenched as he gave Adam an appraising look. "That long, huh?"

"That long, man."

"Hmmph." Dane rubbed his jaw thoughtfully and winced. "Why didn't you say anything?"

"Because he's an idiot!" Bridget socked Adam in the shoulder. "I hate to interrupt your male-bonding moment, but why are you're telling *him* all this stuff that you never told *me?*"

"I, uh, I didn't want to jeopardize my friendship with your brothers, and your family has been so good to me over the years."

Dane barked out a laugh. "Adam, you moron. Colin and I have been trying to set you up with Bridget for years."

She turned to her brother. "What the hell are you talking about? You never told me that!"

"Well, sure, Bridge. We figured Adam's cool, you know. We met some of those duds you dated and didn't want to get stuck with them in the family. Col's got all the dirt on Adam and we figured we could keep him in line."

"Setting me up with her for years?" Adam looked stunned.

Dane shrugged. "Maybe not when she was eighteen, but when she was older. Sure. Why do you think we were always throwing you two together at

Colin's wedding, his kids' baptisms, practically everything Adam came to?"

She gave her brother an incredulous look. "You call *that* matchmaking? I've seen you take more effort figuring which cow Caesar's going to breed with!"

"Now, Bridge…" Dane raised his hands in a placating gesture.

"I can't believe this!" She turned to Adam and threw her hands up. "Do you believe this? My brothers, the Wisconsin *yentas*."

"Bridge—" Adam started and hastily continued at her narrow glare. "I mean, *Bridget,* I swear, I never knew anything about this. I couldn't tell they were matchmaking, either."

Dane looked insulted. "We wanted to be subtle."

"Since when have you clowns ever been subtle?" she challenged. Her brother started to defend himself, but she cut him off. "Weren't you leaving, Dane?" She walked over to her purse and tossed him her spare key ring. "Call a cab and go sleep at my place. Adam and I have a few things to discuss."

The guys both looked worried. Good.

"Okay, Bridge." Dane backed off and went to grab his things while Adam called a cab. Dane came out of the guest room and made a beeline for the front door. "Call me if she kicks you out, too," he stage-whispered to Adam. Oh, yes, Mr. Subtle.

"Goodbye, Dane." She tapped her foot, waiting.

Once he was gone, she turned to the man who was her boyfriend, her lover, her fantasy for more than half a decade. "You had strong feelings for me this whole time?"

He shrugged helplessly. "I really tried not to, Bridget. You were way too young and I had no idea how to treat a nice girl."

She sauntered toward him, making sure the shirt slipped open. "But I wanted you to treat me like a *bad* girl."

He gulped but shook his head. "And would you still be here pursuing your dream if we'd gotten together when you were nineteen? Or would you have put that aside?"

She stopped. "You're right." She had been so head-over-heels for him she would have discarded her education plans without a second thought. Blushing, she remembered a certain old spiral notebook with *Mrs. Bridget Hale* doodled across several pages. "But what now? Do you still have strong feelings for me?"

Running his fingers through his messy hair, he winced as he found a sore spot from his brawl with Dane. "Yeah, I guess you could call them that." His eyes were almost black with emotion. "Sweetheart, you know it was never just loneliness in the big city or exploring your newfound sexuality, or whatever nonsense we used to excuse what was between us. I knew if I let us get this far, I would be a goner." He swallowed hard. "I love you, Bridget. I think I have since we met six years ago. I didn't do anything about it at first because you were too young, and later I was, well, too stupid."

Her eyes filled with tears and spilled onto her cheeks.

"Oh, hey." He sounded nervous. "I didn't mean to make you cry. You're the first woman I've ever told that to, so I don't exactly know what to expect."

She wiped away the dampness and smiled at him. "Silly, I'm crying because I'm happy. I've loved you forever." She giggled at the joy of it. Adam Hale loved her back. She flung her arms around his neck and he buried his face in her hair, giving a great shudder of relief.

He pulled back and stared at her. "You love me, Bridget?" His eyes carried a lifetime of worry that no one would find him lovable if they really knew him, knew him deep down.

She mentally chastised his horrid parents and nodded. "I always have, and I always will." Kissing the base of his throat, she felt his growing erection push through the thin shirt. A little strategic wiggling made him groan and cup her butt. She twirled a lock of springy chest hair around her finger and licked his pec. "Love me, Adam."

He took her in his arms with a fluid movement and carried her to the bedroom. "I always will."

Epilogue

"AND NOW, Richard's on Rodeo presents its newest and hottest exclusive lingerie collection—*Brigitte!*" Richard gestured to the stagehand, who pulled open the curtain to reveal several buxom models in Bridget's creations.

A great cheer and volley of camera flashes from the L.A. fashion media popped in front of Bridget's eyes. She clutched Richard's hand as he grinned and mugged for the cameras. Although she knew he was the undisputed pro at this publicity stuff, she did her best to copy him. She had learned so much from Richard over the past fifteen months as they worked together to bring out her debut collection.

Adam had been able to travel with her here to L.A. a couple times while she worked with Richard's other designers on fine-tuning her bras and panties for mass production by their overseas factory. Despite her grueling schedule, she was still maintaining her excellent grades.

When the spots faded from her vision, she blew

a kiss to Adam, who had a front row seat. Compared to Richard's Southern California flashiness, Adam was the epitome of masculine grace in his classic charcoal suit and blue silk tie. She'd sewn the tie herself from another remnant from her favorite blue cocktail dress.

Adam winked at her. Of all the wonderful things that had happened to her, the absolute best had been falling in love with him and learning he loved her, too.

He looked even more handsome and relaxed now that he had switched to a job as a financial analyst specializing in agricultural economics. She knew he sometimes missed the adrenaline rush of the trading pit, but neither missed his high blood pressure.

She left the photographers clicking away at the gorgeous, scantily clad models and made her way to where Adam stood with her family. Cows or no cows, this time she had made it clear what a big deal this was for her, and they had made arrangements for help at their farms while they traveled to Southern California.

Her male relatives were a hoot. Dane, being single, watched the models avidly. Colin had to content himself with surreptitious peeks when Jenna wasn't looking, and if her poor father blushed any harder, his ears would start smoking.

She threaded her arm through Adam's and he

kissed her cheek, like he always did in front of her parents. "Great job, Bridget."

"Thank you." She thought, *what the heck,* and planted a big kiss on his mouth. He kissed her back but pulled away hastily when Dane cleared his throat menacingly. He was still touchy about walking in on them last year.

"I'm so glad you all came." She gave everyone hugs and kisses, especially her mom. "Thanks for teaching me how to sew."

"Your dad and I are very proud of you, honey." Her mom watched one model pass by. "Maybe I should get you to design something pretty for me."

"My pleasure." Maybe a nice lingerie wardrobe for when she and Dad had more time to lounge around. Adam and her father had discussed the possibility of Adam taking over a smaller version of the farm when her parents did decide to retire. Bridget would be more established in her career and could telecommute from Wisconsin, traveling when necessary.

"Go on, give your present to her." Colin elbowed Adam in the ribs. "I wanna see."

"Colin," his wife teased him. "You're worse than the kids!"

"You bought me a present?" Bridget grabbed Adam's arm.

"Yes, I did. Thanks, buddy." He gave her brother

an exasperated look and drew a long, black velvet jewelry box from his pocket.

Her heart jumped at the sight of it.

She cautiously cracked the box open and gasped. A huge diamond solitaire pendant lay on the lining, suspended from a slender golden chain. "You got me a diamond?" Jenna and her mother crowded in and gave twin exclamations of approval.

She hastily slipped off her beaded choker necklace and let Adam fasten the diamond around her neck. "It's beautiful. Thank you, honey."

He bent in close and whispered for her ears only, "As soon as you say the word, we'll choose an engagement ring to put it in. I love you so much."

She smiled at him. "I love you, too." He smiled back and took her in his arms. Everything was perfect, especially when Adam bent her backward with the sweet power of his kiss. So many things she had hoped for had come to pass when she moved to Chicago, but the best of all was Adam. Adam, friend in her past, lover in her present and husband in her future. Bridget and Adam had made it after all.

HARLEQUIN®

is proud to present

Because sex doesn't have to be serious!

Don't miss the next red-hot title...

PRIMAL INSTINCTS

by

Jill Monroe

Ava Simms's sexual instincts take over as she puts her theories about mating to the test with gorgeous globe-traveling journalist Ian Cole. He's definitely up for the challenge—but is she?

On sale February 2008 wherever books are sold.

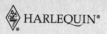

REQUEST YOUR FREE BOOKS!

2 FREE NOVELS PLUS 2 FREE GIFTS!

HARLEQUIN®

Blaze®

Red-hot reads!

Texas Hold 'Em

When it comes to love, the stakes are high

Sixteen years ago, Luke Chisum dated
Becky Parker on a dare…before going
on to break her heart. Now the former
River Bluff daredevil is back, rekindling
desire and tempting Becky to pick up
where they left off. But this time she has
to resist or Luke could discover the secret
she's kept locked away all these years….

Look for

TEXAS BLUFF

by *Linda Warren*

#1470

Available February 2008
wherever you buy books.

You can lead a horse to water...

When Alyssa Barkley and Clint Westmoreland found out that their "fake" marriage was never rendered void, they are forced to live together for thirty days. However, Clint loves the single life and has no intention of being tamed, but when Alyssa moves in, the sizzling attraction between them is ignited and neither wants the thirty days to end.

Look for

TAMING CLINT WESTMORELAND

by

BRENDA JACKSON

Available February wherever you buy books

h

12/09 c

HARLEQUIN®

Blaze™

COMING NEXT MONTH

#375 TEX APPEAL Kimberly Raye, Alison Kent, Cara Summers
A sizzling Valentine collection—Texas-style!
Ride 'em, cowboys! Take a super-hot former rodeo star, a lust-worthy down-home boy and a randy Ranger, mix well with three Southern ladies who are each in need of a little action between the sheets, and what do you get? Tons of *Tex* appeal!

#376 MY WILDEST RIDE Isabel Sharpe
The Martini Dares, Bk. 4
Seduce the man you most desire? That's one tough dare for vulnerable Lindsay Beckham. But she can't resist hot bartender Denver Langston, a man known for serving up delicious cocktails…like Sex on the Beach.

#377 SHAMELESS Tori Carrington
Extreme
Torn between two lovers… Kevin Webster, Patrick Gauge and Nina Leonard are business partners and the best of friends. They share everything, including their sexual exploits. So when Nina complains about sleeping alone, Gauge and Kevin set her up with a stranger for a night of incredible anonymous sex. Only, the man in Nina's bed is no stranger….

#378 PRIMAL INSTINCTS Jill Monroe
Blush
Ava Simms's feminine instincts take over as she puts her theories about mating to the test with gorgeous journalist Ian Cole…who's definitely up for the challenge. But will he satisfy Ava's sexual curiosity?

#379 YOUR BED OR MINE? Kate Hoffmann
The Wrong Bed
Caley Lambert is making some changes. She's just dumped her boyfriend, and she's thinking about ditching her job. But she needs time to think, and attending a family wedding at the old lake house seems like the perfect solution. Only, waking up in bed with her first love isn't exactly what she was expecting….

#380 BURNING UP Sarah Mayberry
A month in a luxury location cooking for one man…it's the perfect job. But when Sophie Gallagher agrees to be actor Lucas Grant's chef, she's so not falling for his charm…until he pursues her with delicious intent, that is. And she discovers he is the hottest man alive!

www.eHarlequin.com

HBCNM0108